LUNA DARKNESS

BOOK 4 OF THE LUNA RISING SERIES (A PARANORMAL SHIFTER ROMANCE SERIES)

SARA SNOW

XAVIER

a wolf's first shift was the most painful. Some wolves took hours to complete their first shift and then a few more years before they could transform into their final form. Contrary to the way we were portrayed in movies, most werewolves could actually shift into two different forms. In the first and easier form, we appeared like normal wolves and walked on four legs, except we're about three times larger than your average wolf. In our final form, our pure werewolf form, we shifted to wolf appearance but walked upright on two legs.

We don't shift to our pure werewolf form often because it would be better for a human to accidentally see an over-grown wolf than a hairy wolf-like creature on two legs.

As I stepped forward, my paw print sank into the earth. I kept my head close to the ground as I tracked the scent of my quarry. I looked over at my dad, his dusty brown coat lighter than mine.

He snorted and shook his head.

I stopped walking and called on The Change. I sank my

front claws into the earth and winced as my bones snapped and realigned into my final form. Since we were hunting deep in the forest, the chances of running into a human here were slim.

I rose to my feet in my pure werewolf form, my long arms hanging at my sides. Shifting to our final form put a mental strain on the human part of our minds. Fighting in this form might leave a wolf more at risk, if they weren't one with the change. It took years to master, and not all wolves could achieve it. Once mastered, shifting into one's final form was more freeing than turning into our wolves.

Spreading my arms wide, I closed my eyes to take a moment to enjoy it. This final form was the form that made us real werewolves.

I turned to follow the scent again, leaving my dad behind as he changed as well. The further I walked, the stronger the smell became. My head snapped to the side, my ears twitching, and I turned left.

Closer...I was getting closer.

Even with my massive body, I moved silently through the underbrush. When I finally caught up to my target, I crouched low, the claws on my feet sinking into the earth, as I prepared to strike.

My prey looked up warily while sensing my presence, as her innocent eyes cautiously studied the forest around her.

I concealed myself in the dark shadow of a large tree.

Before she could meander away, I attacked, rushing forward rapidly to sink my claws into her massive body. My canine fangs sank deeply into flesh, the taste of blood coating my lips as I snapped the doe's neck with ease.

I sat back, blood dripping from my claws as I removed

them from the now dead deer. I stared down at the animal, her lifeless brown eyes still open. I remembered the look of raw fear in her eyes as I had attacked. Being a werewolf could sometimes be a taxing fight between the human and the wolf. It was easier for me to kill a supernatural that had been hurting others rather than an innocent animal like this doe. Something bothered me about hunting like this—not that I'd ever tell anyone. All wolves must learn to hunt, but killing was something I'd never enjoyed. The animals looked at us the same way a human would, with fear and confusion about what we were. Whether they were animals or humans, to our prey, we looked like twisted, horrible versions of the wolves they knew.

I guess some humans might be able to relate to how I felt. I'd noticed some of them seemed to like their animals more than their fellow human beings.

I picked up the lifeless deer to carry under one arm and headed back. Extra werewolf strength did come in handy when it came time to bring dinner home with you. I met up with my dad, who was carrying another deer. Together, we returned to the pack, maintaining our pure werewolf forms for as long as possible.

Before long, we arrived at a small clearing in the forest filled with countless spacious green tents. At the center of the clearing sat a three-story house. This small clearing area and the house within it represented our pack's temporary living arrangements since the vampires launched their attack on the living world three weeks ago. Humans, werewolves, witches, and every living creature with blood flowing through its veins were now prey to these bloodsuckers.

When we arrived, Dad and I gave the deer to Randoll, our

pack's beta. He would arrange for the animals to be cleaned and cooked. In one of the outdoor showers we created for the camp, I shifted back into human form and got dressed. The men slept outside in the tents while our women and children slept inside the protection of the house. All we knew of the chaos happening outside our little forest sanctuary came from whatever Axel and Reika could tell us.

My legs froze mid-walk as the rhythmic sound of a helicopter drew close.

More and more wolves stopped what they're doing to look up at the sky.

Suddenly, the fearful cry of a small child pulled my attention. I turned around.

Little Jasmine was clinging to her mother, her little arms wrapped around Amera's neck tightly. Her cherry blonde hair matching her mother's, messy and tangled. Her mother tried to soothe her, but the child only kept crying.

Around us, other children were running to their fathers' tents or clinging to their mothers.

I ambled over to the wailing girl and tapped her arm gently as the noise of the helicopter drew closer and closer, louder and louder. "Hey," I greeted her.

She peeked at me with one cheek on her mother's shoulder.

"Don't be scared. You're safe here," I assured her.

She shook her head and sniffled as she hid her face again.

"Hey, look, I'll prove it."

She peeked at me again, her petite body now shaking.

I pointed at the helicopter as it finally flew over us. "See."

She leaned up and wiped her nose with the back of her

hand. Her tiny brows knitted as she searched the sky for the helicopter.

"It's gone. They can't see us down here," I whispered to the child.

She raised a brow. "How?" she asked, her voice a delicate squeak.

"My friend had a witch cast a spell on this place. All that they can see from up there..." I pointed to the sky. "...are trees."

"The humans won't see the camp?" she asked in disbelief.

I shook my head with a smile as I used my thumb to wipe away a fat teardrop on her cheek.

She glanced at her mother for confirmation, still doubting the veracity of my words.

Her mother nodded.

The girl started smiling, "Okay."

"Okay, dry your tears," I urged. "Do you like eating deer? I'll make sure you get as much as you like for dinner. Okay?"

Her smile grew as color returned to her pale face. "Thank you."

"Thank you, Xavier, thank your father—" the child's mother started to say, but her face fell as she looked past me.

The silence among the pack that had been present when the helicopter passed overhead returned, and I wondered why. I turned around to see Ruby standing behind me.

She smiled at Jasmine, who then hid her face again.

I frowned, my anger bubbling to the surface as I looked around me to see everyone staring at Ruby. "Ruby," I called.

She sighed and turned away, but she didn't stop.

I watched her hurry back to the house, and I clenched my

fists to stop myself from losing my cool. "She's not a threat," I stated as calmly as I could to Amera.

Jasmine now clung to Amera tightly in fear. She placed the child on the ground, but Jasmine still attached herself to her leg. "We know she's your mate, Xavier. We all also know you don't really know if she's a threat or not. She killed vampires with her bare hands."

"Yes, *vampires*," I said, emphasizing the vampires. Three weeks ago, Ruby had burned two vampires to a crisp without even touching them. After that and perhaps because of that, she was in a coma for three days. By the time she awoke, there wasn't a man, woman, or child in the Blackmoon Pack who didn't know exactly who Ruby was and what she had done to those vampires. The rumor somehow spread to other packs before we could contain it.

Of course, the story managed to make it all the way to the Council. Once the Council learned of what she had done, they predictably wanted her for themselves. In their infinite wisdom, the Council put out a contract for her capture and delivery, endangering all of us.

Our entire pack had to move to a different location to protect her. Axel was able to provide this more secure site. I wasn't happy about the fact that Ruby was his mate as well, but I couldn't deny that he'd been helpful. The man was well-prepared, I'd give him that.

Amera merely gave me a look filled with pity. "Her scent has changed, Xavier. She's not human, and we're not sure what she is. Yes, she killed vampires, but she did so by accident. She didn't know what she was doing. No one here wants to *accidentally* end up as her next victim."

There wasn't much I could say back to her, so I turned on my heels and stormed away.

Ruby had already vanished back inside the house.

The wolves in my pack were my people, my family, but Ruby was my mate. I couldn't stand by and watch them treat her like this. She was my mate, which also meant she was the Luna to be for our pack. Human or not, I had and always would accept her for who she was, whatever she was.

Ruby accepted me being a werewolf. Now, when the tables were turned, I couldn't turn my back on her.

Even so, Ruby had been keeping to herself as of late. She hardly spoke anymore, and I could see that she was clearly losing weight. I felt her putting up a wall between us, and I'd had enough of it.

Ruby

I shouldn't have gone outside.

I heard the helicopter and wanted to see what was happening, even though I knew we were hidden under the masking spell over our pack's area. I recognized that I'd been isolating myself lately. It was the price I had to pay, to avoid the scared or judgmental looks like the ones I'd just received.

With many women and kids staying inside the house, my room was usually my only available escape. As I walked by the living room on the way to my room, I realized that for once,

7

it was empty. I went in and closed the sliding double doors. I would probably have it to myself for a while now. Once they smelled me in here, no one else would want to come in.

This led to another question. *Why has my scent changed?*

I'd grown sick of the tests Natalie performed without a witch's help. So far, none of her tests revealed what my supernatural lineage was. There had to be some kind of a supernatural explanation for me to have done what I did.

Magic was there, flowing through my body, but it wasn't the kind of magic Natalie had ever seen. Reika and Willow had been unable to come to us since the world had fallen into chaos. During the first week, vampires and humans fought hard against each other. This battle was just the beginning of this nightmare. The situation only worsened the second week when humans discovered werewolves existed. Then the humans turned on us as well, just as the wolves always feared.

I snorted as I crossed my arms and stared out the window. I had finally accepted I was a part of the supernatural world, the werewolf community specifically, by way of my mates. Then, just that fast, the world went to hell, and I was back to square one. After I burned those vamps from the inside out, it seemed like I wasn't even an accepted part of the werewolf community anymore, either.

The door opened, but I didn't bother looking. I knew it was either Natalie, Xavier, or Mathieu. They were the only people who would speak to me anymore.

"Ruby?" Xavier called softly.

I sighed and glanced his way.

"Talk to me," he said.

"They're all terrified of me."

He joined me at the window and leaned against it as he watched me.

I avoided looking at him. I was barely holding it together as it was, and gazing into his eyes would just make me fall apart. "I don't blame them." I looked down at my hands. "I'm terrified of me."

He reached out and held my hands as he guided me to stand before him. "We'll find out what's going on, and we'll do it together. I'll always be there for you, no matter what. Please don't forget that."

I reached out and cupped his cheek. I knew I had been misbehaving towards him, but I'd needed space. "I'm sorry for shutting you out too. I've just been so tired, Xavier." My hand fell away from his cheek to pinch the bridge of my nose. "What's happening to me?" My hand fell to my side limply, and I hung my head.

His hands slid around my waist. I sighed as I stepped forward to press my body to his. He reached up to gently caress my hair as I lost myself in the warmth emitting from his body.

"Everyone is just confused and scared and not just because of you," he spoke softly. "So much is happening right now. Wolves are dying by the thousands. Not to mention the humans are being picked off one by one by the vampires. These vampires are adding more and more to their ranks nightly. Soon, there will be too many of them, and a battle with them will be futile." He turned his head to the side. "While wolves that can help to save this world are trapped in hiding because humans think we're the same as those things."

I leaned back to look up at him. "But why is the Council refusing to reach out to the humans?" I questioned. "Why not try to come together to defeat a common enemy? Right now, humans are basically helping vampires." I shook my head at the sheer stupidity. "They're so fucking stupid, stretching their resources to kill werewolves that aren't attacking them when they are being murdered in the streets by vampires." I stepped away from him. "Will they do the same when they find out about witches, or demons, not to mention everything else supernatural? This war will never end!"

Xavier held my arm and guided me to the sofa to sit down. "Right now, it's every species for themselves. It's fucked up, but I think right now, everyone is in shock and is just trying to survive. The wolves out there are scared - terrified even - because no one knows what's coming next."

Something has to be done.

Xavier had said it himself that the vampires were turning more and more humans and supernaturals. With everyone selfishly caring for only themselves, people were being picked off by the vamps more easily. There was strength in numbers, so the humans and supernatural community were divided. Humans didn't even know about the existence of some of the other supernatural creatures yet.

It was just like in a horror movie when every person went their own separate way. Inevitably, they would just be picked off one by one by the evil entity.

"After this…" He rolled his eyes. "…if there is even an *after*, the Council will have no hold on the wolf community. Not after they've left us without help," he stated with a bitter edge in his voice. "The Council has ways and means of protecting the community. Many packs were thankful for the information we sent them about the vampires. Some didn't even know about the vampires."

Natalie came into the room quietly as he finished.

I sighed when I saw her.

"I know, but we need to get back to testing," Natalie insisted as she walked over to us and sat on the arm of the sofa.

"I'm not ready. Just give me a minute," I replied.

"I know this is exhausting," she said. "But we have to do what we have to do. Let's be real here. You don't know what powers you have. We know next to nothing about your magic. All we do know is the shitty situation we're in is only going to get worse."

I heard her implication loud and clear. Every day it took for us to get answers, the risk rose that someone in the pack would hand me over to the humans or the Council. The pack had been uprooted and moved because of me. Men were sleeping outside because there was no space. There was precious little food and water for everyone. In their view, I was just a ticking time bomb, a safety risk for all involved.

I'd been trying not to think about that night. I think the searing white-hot pain I felt before falling unconscious might have been a tiny pinch of what those incinerated vampires felt. While they deserved it, it was excruciating. I couldn't let that happen here. "Okay," I replied

Xavier got up to give Natalie his seat.

I sighed. "I really hate this."

Natalie smiled with empathy, "I know, so do I."

I gazed over at Xavier.

He watched us, his shirt pulling taut over his chest as he crossed his arms.

I looked back at Natalie and nodded.

She placed her hands on my head, preparing to try and

break through the barrier in my mind as she had been attempting repeatedly for the past three weeks.

It was exhausting for both of us, and so we were only able to do it twice a week. So far, she had only been able to see quick glimpses of my past that offered no kind of assistance or understanding. Sometimes, I saw what she did. Other times, I saw nothing at all.

"Wait." I suddenly pulled away.

Natalie's hands fell onto her lap.

My eyes darted from her to Xavier and back. "I can't, not right now."

She exhaled heavily through her mouth and pressed a finger at the crease between her brows. "Okay. If Reika were here, this wouldn't be as bad. Unfortunately, she can't leave Romania right now, with everything that has been happening." She gave me a sad smile before she addressed Xavier. "Have you spoken to Axel? He had a witch he was going to contact. I don't know how much more of this Ruby or I can take. It's pointless putting each other under this strain when it's barely working."

"I know," Xavier agreed softly. "I spoke to him and his pack is finally secure. The Council tried to get him to turn Ruby over. He hasn't been able to contact her, and he's not sure when he'll be able to come here."

"We can try again tomorrow, Natalie," my voice was a whisper as I stood up. Axel's pack had to move as well because of me, and I hadn't even been there. My existence was becoming a burden to everyone around me.

It was hard not to feel bad for myself when the world was falling apart and I was just adding fuel to the fire. For now, I just wanted to sleep. Sleeping was an escape from this place, being the only time I felt at peace. Well, as long as I didn't dream about those vampires I incinerated, anyways. "I'm feeling tired, guys. I'm going to go to bed early. Okay?" I gave Xavier a half-smile that was barely even a facial tick.

Natalie stood up, caressed my cheek tenderly, and then nodded.

I turned away quickly, my eyes stinging with tears even as I made my way to my room.

2

RUBY

A few days after we moved to this location, I wandered off into the forest seeking a little peace away from the chaos of our living situation. Eventually, I stumbled upon the most peaceful and surreal view.

I found a hill that overlooked a part of the forest covered with flowers along with trees scattered about them. Woodland animals would wander by me, uncaring that I was there. To me, this felt as close as I'd ever get to finding the Garden of Eden.

The large rock that sat perfectly atop the hill served as my not-so-cushioned spot to sit for hours on end.

Since I hadn't been up to it last night, Natalie and I had mind-linked this morning. Of course, yet again, we learned nothing new. All I saw was a glimpse of myself when I was about fifteen years old. I was getting into a cab, a broad smile on my face as I waved goodbye to someone. Then the vision abruptly ended.

Despite the short duration of the vision, I did manage to

pick out a few important clues. For one thing, I noticed my hair was shorter, to my shoulder, whereas now it was at my waist. It was also a much darker dyed red as opposed to my lighter natural shade now. Considering I've never dyed my hair before, the change in hair color really stood out. Also, who would I wave to with such a beaming smile? People annoyed me—they always had. My dislike for people in general combined with the lack of a filter between my mind and my mouth meant not many people ended up really getting who I was. This was the main reason I'd felt shocked when I clicked with Natalie so quickly. It was rarer still to earn a genuine smile from me, and such smiles were generally reserved for only the people I cared most about. To earn a smile of that caliber from me, whomever I was waving at must have been important to me. Whomever this mystery person was, I clearly cared about them.

Since I avoided eating in the kitchen or dining room with everyone else, I ate the last of my sandwich in my special spot. Even with my bleak childhood as a foster kid, I've never felt more like an outcast. Feeling alone in a crowd was indeed worse than feeling that way by oneself.

The wind picked up, causing my crimson hair to dance around me as I closed the container on my lap and placed it on the ground beside me. I bent my legs to wrap my hands around my knees and inhaled the sweet smell of flowers drifting in the breeze.

A twig snapped behind me, and it startled me. I swung around and almost fell off the rock in the process. My eyes widened as I came face to face with a jet-black wolf.

He stood a few steps away from me, his mouth ajar as he panted rapidly.

I swallowed nervously as my heart began to hammer in my chest.

Xavier's coat was brown, and I had never noticed a black wolf within the pack. Then again, I hadn't seen all the wolves in their shifted form. Was this a pack member about to kill me? Was this an outsider that had come to turn me over to the Council?

I didn't move and kept my gaze straight into the eyes of the wolf. "Who are you?" I asked, surprised at how steady my voice sounded.

The wolf closed its mouth and stopped panting as his black eyes changed to hazel.

I narrowed my eyes and scrunched my face as my brows furrowed tightly. "Axel?"

The wolf snorted and stepped forward confidently.

I exhaled through my mouth, relieved. "You seriously scared me there for a minute."

He padded over to me.

In my seated position, he towered over me like a mountain. I remained motionless as his cold nose brushed against my warm cheek. I reached up to softly touch the side of his face. I smiled shyly as my finger sank into his silky fur.

He tilted his head softly towards my touch.

His obsidian coat was indescribably beautiful. I wouldn't tell him this, but I was happy he was here. We could be outsiders together.

He pulled away suddenly, walked away, and vanished in the trees. He shifted and returned a few minutes later.

I quickly averted my eyes when I caught a glimpse of his abs as he pulled his shirt down. The last thing I wanted was for him to catch me checking him out. He'd never let me forget it.

His dark curly hair hung loose around his shoulders and messy. The corner of his mouth arched knowingly as he walked over to me and crouched down. "My wolf looks great, right? I know," he joked.

This earned him an exaggerated eye roll from me.

He chuckled as he stared at the forest and stood. He then carefully sat down on the rock beside me.

"You're so full of yourself," I teased him. "You shouldn't have come," I told him seriously.

He shrugged nonchalantly then turned to look at me. "Yeah, I missed you too."

"That's not what I said," I replied quickly.

He used a hand to comb his hair backward casually and stared at me for a moment, his hazel eyes somehow appearing lighter than I remembered them. "You don't need to say it."

Like always, his intense gaze made my heart flutter. I averted my eyes, unable to look at him any longer. In my peripheral vision, I could see he was still focused intently on me, his eyes roaming all over my body.

Stop fucking looking at me like that, dammit!

Neither of us spoke for a moment, and my mind started to wander.

Then, with concern evident in his voice, he whispered to me, "What happened?"

I deliberately avoided his eyes and directed my gaze to the forest floor before the rock. He was asking about the one thing I didn't want to talk about, the one thing I didn't have an answer for. I bit down on my lip as I watched a small insect fly from one flower to another. I recalled the witch from the shop Xavier and I had gone to who had told us she could go to another world. Right now, I fervently wished I could do the same. "I don't know," I finally answered. "I just reacted."

I glanced up at him to gauge his reaction. I feared he might regard me with the same fear and suspicion as the rest of the pack. To my relief, all I saw on his face was concern for me. My lips formed a thin line as I looked away from him, looking to my left to avoid him seeing the pain and sadness in my eyes. I welcomed his kindness. I didn't get much of it from anyone else other than Xavier, Mathieu and Natalie, but Axel would see more than I wanted him to.

"Did you speak to the witch who made the scent-masking potions?" I inquired, "Can she help me?" The sound of him brushing his hand down his pants made me look his way once more.

"I did. She can't help, but she recommended someone that can."

I sensed a 'but' coming, and there was no room for that. If there was someone who could get through the barrier in my mind, I wanted it done. "But?"

"He's a warlock that practices dark magic."

"Is that really as bad as you're making it seem? If he can help, I want to go to him," I stated.

His chest rose and fell as he inhaled and exhaled deeply.

I arched a brow as he took his sweet time to respond. "Axel?"

"Yes, it's as bad as it sounds. Black magic shouldn't be taken lightly. There is a price to pay for using it. Maybe we'll get lucky and the warlock will be willing to bear the cost of the black magic in exchange for some other form of compensation. However, if you must pay, then that's a problem."

My mouth turned downward as I shrugged. "What's the price?"

"I don't know what the price will be for doing this, but when you think of black magic, think of necromancy. Necromancy is strong magic but comes with a price only a few are willing to pay. You lose a piece of your soul with each life you bring back. Black magic is the same but with countless prices, from taking a life down to losing a hand."

"Okay, then," I drawled.

Axel narrowed his eyes. "Okay. Would you still want the warlock's help if the price is never to have children?"

I grimaced. "Okay, I get it. But we don't know the price. Maybe it won't be anything that drastic. I want to do it. Natalie alone can't help me. The sooner we know what I am and what's in my past, the better."

"I can't say I know how you feel," he said thoughtfully, his voice deep and gravelly. "I was born a wolf. I've known what I am since birth."

I shot him a look that told him just how little he was helping my mood.

He smiled and held a hand up. "What I can tell you is this... whatever you are, Ruby, own it. Nothing good will come from trying to suppress who you really are. Denying or suppressing your powers will only throw you off balance. A wolf who fights the change during their first shift only ends up suffering unnecessarily." He gently reached out and held a strand of my hair the way as is becoming his habit.

To my surprise, I found his sage words to be comforting. I

understood what he was saying entirely, but it was easier said than done.

"Trust me," he added.

Do I? Do I trust him?

He stared at me and released my hair. "There's a full moon tomorrow night. That's why I came. If there is an attack, my people are safe. Even with the cloaking spell, you guys are still at risk. You need all the protection you can get."

I tried not to overthink how he had risked himself and his pack by coming here just for me. "How are you so sure your pack is safe without you? How is your father doing, by the way?"

He began rubbing his finger back and forth on his chin as he stared up at a bird soaring in the sky above us. "He's doing better, thanks. I know my pack is safe because there are three witches there, plus the warlock you met. With all their warding and cloaking spells, my people have the best protection possible."

I turned completely to face him.

He looked me up and down as if wondering what I was doing.

I leaned forward, and my eyes lowered into slits. "What's up with you and all these witch friends, huh? I thought werewolves and witches didn't mix."

He shrugged nonchalantly. "I was in love with a witch, once."

I pulled back, my eyes widening somewhat. That was not at all what I'd expected to hear. The fact that he said it so casually seemed to be a testament to how far he and I had come in our relationship. When we first met, if I asked a single question, he'd bite my head off. Now, we were sitting outside together, companionably sharing sensitive information about ourselves.

I smiled inwardly. To be honest, it was nice talking to him. "Oh, I'm going to need a little more than that." I grinned.

He chuckled softly. "Of course, you wouldn't be you if you didn't."

I smacked his arm. "Are you calling me nosy? Because I am." I giggled.

He laughed along with me, but his laughter was short-lived. "Obviously, I wasn't mated to her, but we loved each other." His jaws clenched. "I loved her. My pack couldn't know about us, but her coven was aware of our relationship. Her people didn't approve, of course. I think my dad knew about her, but he never said anything. Believe it or not, when I was younger, I didn't want to be Alpha."

"That's shocking," I grumbled.

He laughed as he nodded. "Yeah, but it's true. My mother was alive then, and I was hoping she'd have another son who would want to take the title of Alpha. Although, I'm the first-born...but that's another story." He combed his hair back lazily and closed his eyes as he scratched at his scalp.

I found myself wondering what his hair would feel like if I reached out and touched it. He was always feeling mine.

He went on, "When a demon killed the witch I loved, I helped her coven to avenge her death. They welcomed me after that." He snorted and lowered his hand. He stared off in the distance, a crease between his brows. "Funny, how it was her death that made us allies. We later found out the demon that killed her was working for a human."

My heart sank. This explained a lot about Axel's hatred

towards humans. One of them was responsible for the death of the woman he'd loved. "I'm really sorry, Axel."

He accepted my words with a brief nod. "So, the witches I know that I can call on for help are all from her coven."

I bit down on my lips and heaved a sigh. I wasn't sure what to think now. A human killed his first love, and now he ended up mated to one. I scrunched my face. *Then again, I might not be human.*

"What?" he asked.

I shook my head slowly. "Nothing. I guess I understand now why you hate humans so much and why you were so upset to be mated to one."

He held my gaze for a moment. "Yes, that's why I hate humans and why I never fell in love with anyone after her."

Well, this is awkward.

"But I don't hate you, Ruby," he added quickly, "Plus, you're not human." His eyes roamed over my face and hair, as if he saw something no one else could. "You weren't from the start. We just need to find out what you actually are."

I folded my lips. "What if I'm some lab rat, some human experiment gone wrong? Or some messed up hybrid? I don't want to hurt any of you. You guys are all I have." The words were out of my mouth before I could stop myself.

Axel didn't hide his surprise either. His face smoothed out as he smiled at me and he reached up to give my chin a quick pinch. "Don't worry about that, Red. We're in this together. You're my mate, remember? We'll figure it out together. I don't abandon my family, so like it or not, you're stuck with me."

3

RUBY

*M*y eyes started to twitch, causing me to press my fingers against them. The twitching stopped, but my eyes slowly started to become blurry until I no longer saw the forest before me.

A white wolf growled at me, its mouth cavernous and its fluffy tail swished from side to side. I watched as the wolf was engulfed by black smoke and a distorted monstrous growl pierced the air. A giant cobra appeared out of the smoke, slithering from side to side. It flicked its tongue at the sky before rising, hood now showing as it hissed.

I stared at long fangs painted red as my head fell back to properly look up at the snake.

The cobra swayed, his movements almost hypnotizing, then it whipped its head forward in the blink of an eye to strike me.

I jumped and grabbed onto the rock beneath me before I almost fell off. I blinked my eyes rapidly as I looked around me. I was back in the forest at my spot.

I sighed as I pressed my fingers into my eyes. This was the sixth time I'd had that vision since the incident when I burned the vampire. No matter how many times I saw it...it always got me. Tonight would be the full moon and all the wolves were on edge. I'd been out here in the woods since daybreak in an attempt to avoid the other pack members.

Tensions were running high, and I'd rather not have someone finally decide to take their frustrations out on me. Sighing, I gulped down the rest of my orange juice and placed it into the paper bag along with the container that held my sandwich.

Placing my hands behind me on the rock, I leaned my head back towards the sky as I closed my eyes. I attempted to relax and focus on the sounds of the forest - the birds, insects, the wind in the trees - anything to take my mind off the images from the vision. It seemed like someone had pressed the repeat button. Each time I got the vision again, it remained stubbornly stuck in my mind to the point where I couldn't concentrate on anything else all day.

I opened my eyes calmly, expecting to see a peaceful blue sky above me. Instead, I found myself looking directly into a pair of emerald green eyes. I let out a scream so high pitched, probably only dogs—or wolves—could hear it and jumped up frantically, ready to bolt. I belatedly realized it was Randoll.

He placed his hands on his knees and started to laugh. "Oh my god, your face!"

I rolled my eyes and clutched at my chest, a smile tugging at the corners of my mouth. Randoll was one of few werewolves who had been nice to me from the start, back when I was just the human in the packhouse. "You're a dick,

Randoll."

He walked forward and flicked his hand at me for me to scoot over. "I know. What are you doing out here?"

I sighed heavily. "I think you know what."

He looked over at me and pursed his lips as he nodded. "Yeah." His red hair was much like mine, but now too long as it covered his forehead.

"You need a haircut," I stated.

He looked up at the strands of hair just above his eyes. "I kind of like it."

"Of course you would," I replied.

He chuckled. "This is cool," he remarked after we sat in silence for a moment. "Nice view."

I nodded in agreement. "It is. Is Xavier looking for me or something?"

He shook his head. "Nah, I...um, was on patrol and smelled you out here."

"Oh," I drawled. I'd have to remember to ask Axel to procure more of the potion to mask my scent. Xavier had tried to reassure me that my new scent wasn't bad. He'd characterized it as 'kind of indescribably sweet.' I still found it very disturbing because there was no way to ignore it like a normal human scent. It was like the constantly delicious smell of fresh bread being made, as Natalie described it.

"How are you doing, Ruby?" Randoll asked as he turned to look at me. "I know the pack is being pretty hard on you right now."

"I'm not doing great, obviously. But as I've said, I can't blame them," I looked down at my hands, at the lines in my palm. "I'm scared of myself too."

"Why?" he asked gently.

I laughed, but it sounded humorless. "I don't know what I am, Randoll. *I do not know what I am.* I don't even know if my real name is Ruby. You have no idea how it feels not to know who you are."

"So, you really don't have any memories from your past?" He probed, his voice low as he leaned over somewhat. "I heard one of the wolves talking. They said Natalie is trying to help you to get them back."

I nodded. "I have memories of my past. Certain memories were just locked away. I can't feel like I've forgotten something if I don't recognize that memory to begin with. Shouldn't you already know this? You're the beta for the pack."

His mouth turned down as he made a face. "Yes, but I'm not told everything. I enforce the alpha's rules and keep the pack in check. Right now, though, everyone is..." He paused and sighed. "Everyone is getting on my nerves."

I could certainly understand that sentiment. While I understood everyone's fear of me, they were treating me as if I had the plague. It got old fast.

"What did it feel like?" he suddenly asked.

"What?" I asked, confused.

He pointed to my hands. "What did it feel like when you killed them?"

I used my tongue to poke my cheek out as I gazed up at the blue sky. "I was having odd pains in my body before it happened. With the first vampire, I didn't really feel anything. He just—he just started to burn to death, and then I realized it was because of me." I was seeing the vampire in my head as I spoke. I could see the confusion and pain in his eyes as he died slowly and agonizingly. "When the second vampire attacked me, I only reacted." I threw my hands up to block myself as I had back then. "He was going to kill me. I was in shock. I didn't know what the fuck was happening other than my hands were burning from the inside out. After that vampire died, my power turned on me." I glanced back over at him.

A deep crease had formed between his brows. "That's what happened?"

I frowned. "Yeah, my powers turned on me after I used them."

He combed his hair back, but the wild curls only sprang forward to cover his forehead again. "That's crazy," he murmured under his breath. "You're a walking, talking vampire flame thrower without the flame." His eyes widened as he grinned. "Maybe it's not fire, but more like a kind of radiation."

"I don't get it," I replied.

"Too much radiation burns, doesn't it?"

"I don't know. Trust me, it was like a volcano was bubbling inside me." I clenched and unclenched my fist as I remembered the pain. "I've never felt anything so painful. It was worse than the vampire bite."

"So, you can't tell when it's coming on to like, move away to protect others? It can just...happen?"

I stared at him for a moment.

He stared back at me expectantly.

I realized he wasn't asking me all of these questions because he was concerned. He was only talking to me to find out how unstable I was, to find out if I could be trusted or if I was a threat.

He made a face as the silence stretched on between us. He started to look uncomfortable because of the way I was just staring at him.

"No, Randoll, I can tell. Why are you asking me all of this?"

He laughed sheepishly. "What do you mean, Ruby?"

I got up and stepped away from him. "I'm a fucking moron to think you're any different from the others. Did they send you? Huh? I bet they sent you to talk to me to see what you can learn because Xavier and Mathieu aren't telling you guys anything."

Randoll stood up slowly. "Ruby, I was only trying to understand what's going on. When Axel turned up yesterday, the others started to get angry. We aren't being told anything other than what happened with the vampires and you and that we all need to hide."

I started shaking my head. I could hear the blame in his voice. "They all had to hide because of me, right? Not like they weren't, *we weren't*, all already in hiding or about to be, right? From...I don't know... the vampires? God, you're all fucking full of it. You're all making it seem as if I'm the vampire threat that has started this mess. My life is fucked too, you know! Have any of you thought about that! No one is safe, whether I'm here or not, Randoll! It's only a matter of time before the humans or the vampires find us and that doesn't have to be solely because of me!" As I turned away, an unfamiliar sensation started to pulsate within my body. My heartbeat was hammering in my ears. I closed my eyes as I prayed not to go nuclear, not now.

"Please, Randoll, leave me alone." I could hear his footsteps as he drew closer to me. The closer he got, the more I started to shake, and I realized I felt him there. I felt his energy. I felt the energy in the air, earth, and trees around us. It was like a low hum in my ear, a surprisingly soothing sound.

It wasn't the heat like before. While I felt relieved about that, I was also scared. I didn't know what this new sensation meant. I didn't know what any of this meant. "Go, now, please," I whispered urgently.

"Ruby, I'm sorry, I didn't mean to upset you. Everyone just wants to know what's really going on. No one knows what you are. No one knows what you're capable of. If you're powerful enough to kill a vampire, imagine what you could do to us."

"I would never!" I screamed as I spun around.

Randoll was thrown backward by an unseen force.

I gasped and covered my mouth as he tried to catch his balance but fell backward.

His eyes were wide in shock that certainly matched my surprised ones.

My eyes stung with tears as I looked around us at the flowers, bushes, and twigs that had been blown back. I swallowed hard. My hand shook as it fell from my mouth to hang limply at my side. I could have killed him. I could have done precisely what he and the others were afraid of me doing. "I'm sorry," I whispered as a tear escaped an eye. I backed away from him. "I'm so sorry."

Randoll sat up. "Ruby, don't," he said.

I still turned and ran.

Xavier

*I*t wasn't hard to find her. I followed her scent through the forest until I found her sitting under a tree, a curious squirrel sitting in front of her.

Ruby held her hand out and the little critter moved forward instead of away from her. She cocked her finger, her soothing voice vibrating as she tried to lure the small animal in.

It came closer and closer until it could smell the tips of her finger before running away and then back to her.

I smiled as she giggled.

The squirrel ran off when he noticed my arrival.

She sighed as she noticed me, too. She got to her feet quickly and turned, walking away.

It only took me a few long strides to catch up to her. "So," I drawled. "Are you leaving then?"

She stopped and turned to look at me, her brows furrowed with rage.

I sobered up. "I was kidding."

"Of course you were, because you know there is nowhere I can actually go. I'm stuck in a place where no one wants me, and I'm putting everyone in danger."

"That's not true," I replied.

She gave me a flat look.

"It's not true that *no one* wants you here," I corrected myself. "And you know that."

She continued walking.

I strolled by her side silently. A contrite Randoll had found me and sheepishly told me what happened with her. She was getting more powerful, that much was clear. I had noticed it from the moment I caught her trail. Her scent was even more potent than before.

Whatever was awakening inside her became stronger each time she used her powers. She had an episode triggered by an argument. It was a risk to have her around everyone, but what other choice was there?

Axel and I had already discussed the possibility of using black magic, and he knew I was completely against it. Black magic was tricky and risky. It was a chance I didn't want to take. Of course, Ruby was ready to do it, but she was still new to this world and did not truly understand the cost.

"Do you sometimes wonder what's happening out there?" she asked. "What's happening with the war while we hide in these woods?"

"Everyone is hiding, I think," I guessed as I nodded. "I want to be out there fighting, helping to save this world, but we're being hunted by humans, werewolves, and those leeching vampires. Going out there means certain death, Ruby, but..."

Pausing, she raised a brow at me.

"I know what's happening to you right now is hard to deal with," I went on. "We will find out what's hidden in your mind and what your powers mean. Once we know all of that and once you can control your gifts, we can get out of here and bring the fight to the vamps."

A small smile curved her lips as she kept walking. "I'd like that."

My heart warmed to see her smiling, but it vanished as soon as it appeared.

"If things turn out that way, that is," she added. "We don't even know enough about what's happening out there to know what we're really up against."

"I spoke to Axel yesterday when he arrived," I replied. "The vampires are slaughtering everyone and everything that has blood and a beating heart. They have an actual society, complete with ranks. On the bottom, you have the Bleeders... they're ravenous and bloodthirsty. Blood is like a drug to them. They are more creature-like, incredibly pale and hairless and feast on anything. Then you have the higher-ups."

She stopped walking and turned to me. "What do you mean?"

"You have the Bleeders and the Skins. The Skins are human-like in terms of their reasoning and can control their thirst. Among them, you have generals, no doubt very powerful. Then you have the queen." This was just about all the information Reika had been able to gather from the Council. It wasn't much, but it was enough. "That's why so many people were killed in the first wave. They released the Bleeders to wreak havoc."

"Is there any info on their queen?" she asked.

I shook my head. "Not yet, but Reika said she's working on it. She had also heard some whispers about something but would rather confirm it before saying anything."

Ruby sighed. "Okay, then."

I knew what Ruby was thinking—we still knew very little. However, what I hadn't told Ruby and didn't plan to tell her, was that the Council had doubled its efforts to have her found and captured.

They'd dispatched the Council Guards to hunt her down. It would only be a matter of time before we were located. The Council Guards were an elite group of werewolves, which was why Reika had contacted me through my dreams and not a phone. Even then, she had to limit her contact with us.

Mathieu, Axel, Natalie, and I had been thinking about a way to go about moving Ruby, but so far, all ideas we had come up with had a high probability of failing.

The Council werewolves weren't the only ones that wanted her. The humans did as well, and since we didn't have a human source to give us details on that front, we had no idea what they were planning.

"Xavier?"

I blinked and peered down at her. "Yes?"

"I was asking you if Randoll told you what happened."

I intended to walk off, but she held my wrist. "Yes, he did. Don't worry, he didn't tell anyone else but me. He told me he pushed you too far and you got angry. It's not surprising your rage triggered your powers." I frowned as a thought occurred to me.

Ruby's green eyes roamed my face with worry. "What is it?"

"I think maybe that's what we need to do," I replied as a smile slowly started to stretch my lips. "Why didn't I think of this sooner?"

"I'm not following," she grumbled.

I cupped her chin gently. "We need to push you to use your powers."

She narrowed her eyes at me. "That won't work. I have no idea how to even—I don't know how to make it work, okay? I was scared the first time and angry the second time."

As the wheels in my mind turned, my smile grew wider. "Trust me, what I have in mind will work."

4

RUBY

a drop of sweat dripped into my eye, causing my sight to blur, but I kept running. My heartbeat was pounding in my ears as I ran through the woods, the muscles in my legs now sore and aching. I could hear them behind me, chasing after me as I ran. I forced all my energy into my legs to keep pushing me forward.

A howl echoed through the forest.

I wiped a hand over my forehead as I ran behind a tree and stopped. Pressing my back to its trunk, I tried not to breathe too loudly, but I was exhausted.

I looked down at my right elbow and grimaced at the scratch there from where I had tripped earlier. It wasn't bad, but it was bleeding. As more howls echoed through the forest, I pushed away from the tree and started running again.

I tried to mask my scent as I had done with the vampires. But since my scent had become more robust ever since it changed, I doubted that anything could cover up my smell now. All I'd done was cover myself unnecessarily in dirt and mud.

With it being late afternoon to evening, the sun still shone through the canopy of trees above, something I felt thankful for since I could see where I was running. It hadn't stopped me from tripping earlier. Nor did it prevent me from tripping again, as I stubbed my toe and fell forward.

I bit down on my lip to hold back my scream as I fell, my arms outstretched to cushion my fall. Groaning, I remained on the ground for a few seconds to catch my breath. A twig snapped behind me, and I spun around onto my back.

I swiftly rolled to the side as a dark brown wolf jumped at me, its massive paws coming down hard where I had just been. I got to my feet quickly, my tangled dirty hair covering my face somewhat. I had to duck to the side again, as the wolf charged forward while slashing its claws at me.

I rolled away swiftly and rose to one knee as the animal growled, its black eyes watching me closely. I gripped a stone firmly behind my back as I slowly rose onto my legs.

The wolf stopped pacing a circle around me to snap its jaws in my direction.

I threw the stone suddenly, but the wolf easily dodged it and charged at me. I raised my hand as I tried to use my powers, and the wolf skidded to a halt. I looked at my hand and then the wolf.

Nothing happened. I sighed heavily, and my hand fell limply to my side. "It's not working," I stated the obvious to Xavier.

He made a snorting sound and sat down.

I smiled. "Maybe it's because I know you won't hurt me. Good chase, though."

The enormous paws of a black wolf appeared from behind a tree. It belonged to Axel, the other wolf that had been chasing me. When he fully emerged from behind the trunk, I frowned.

His head was still dipped aggressively and his sharp canine fangs were still on full display.

I glanced at Xavier, who had gotten up, and I threw a look Axel's way when he growled. "It didn't work, Axel. You can stop now."

He snapped his jaws at me with a growl.

My eyes widened as Xavier growled and moved closer to me. "Axel, what are you doing? I told you it didn't work. Stop!"

It didn't seem to matter what I said—he wasn't listening to me. His eyes were still black pits of rage as he snarled.

Xavier answered with a loud growl.

Xavier thought it would be a good idea for Axel and him to chase me as if to hurt me to see if it would trigger my powers. When I first used my powers, I was scared. The second time I was angry. Maybe if they re-created those feelings, I'd be able to access and eventually learn to control my powers. Yet, nothing had happened. No matter how they had howled, growled, and looked as if they might attack me, I knew deep down I wasn't in any real danger.

However, my heart was beating rapidly as I looked at Axel now, and not from the exertion of running either.

He didn't look like he was faking, and it didn't feel like he was either. He looked angry, furious even as he shook his head, his ears flattened to his head.

"Listen," I tried to deflect what was happening. "I'm

exhausted, and we should probably head back to the camp. It's getting late. There is a full moon tonight, remember?"

Axel kept circling Xavier and me.

Xavier lowered his head as he sent a warning growl Axel's way.

Axel raised his head and snarled louder while he bucked forward as if to attack us.

"Axel?" I entreated in a soft voice but jumped when he snapped his jaws at me.

Xavier moved to stand in front of me and then stepped back, using his body to push me backward.

I knew he was telling me to run. I couldn't, though. I was too confused as to why Axel was still pretending he wanted to hurt me. At first, this seemed like a good idea, even a little fun, but Axel was really starting to scare me.

"Shift back, now! Do you hear me, Axel? You're freaking me out. Shift!"

Maybe that had been the wrong thing to say because he quickly lunged at me.

Xavier reacted swiftly, slamming into Axel.

They both fell to the ground.

I watched with wide eyes as they bit and clawed at each other, my skin tingling as my slight fear turned to panic.

This wasn't fake anymore. Watching two wolves big enough to swallow me whole fight, was something I'd never seen before. I felt like this fight had been building up between them from the very start, and I feared it would only end with the death of one of them.

I gasped as Axel bit viciously into Xavier's side, and Xavier howled in pain. My body started to shake as blood sprayed from the wound in Xavier's side.

That's when I turned and ran. I ran past them to head back to the pack, but this time I didn't care about the ache in my legs or the branches grabbing and poking at my skin. I needed to get to Mathieu or Randoll. I had no idea what had gotten into Axel, but if he caught up to me, I felt it in my soul that I would be a dead woman.

Maybe shifting so close to a full moon had been a bad idea. If it hadn't been safe for them to shift, why would they do this, knowing the risk?

Like before with Randoll, I started to feel pulsing energy within and around me. I tried to hold onto the feeling, but it kept fading only to return and then disappear again. I groaned as I pushed forward when something barreled into me, throwing me to the ground.

I landed with an oomph sound and rolled to my back as I heard a contorted growl. I held my head back as I looked up Axel's towering pure werewolf form. Being jet black, unlike the other wolves—he was truly something to look at.

His long-clawed fingers twitched at his side as I pulled myself back on my hands to get away from him. A deep resounding growl met my ears, and I stopped moving.

"Axel, it's Ruby. You need to calm down, okay. You're not hunting me for real, remember?"

He bared his white teeth and took a step towards me.

A chill went through my body. "I swear, Axel, knock it off right now! What the hell do you think you're doing? Are you going to kill me? Huh? Don't force me to hurt you, Axel. I have no control!"

He took another step forward.

Now, a buzzing sound rang in my ears as my fear grew stronger. I could see blood on the tips of Axel's teeth, no doubt from biting Xavier. My heart grew heavy as I remembered Xavier and wondered if he was all right. Had Axel killed Xavier?

This wolf couldn't be Axel. It couldn't be. Why would Axel turn on us like this? Why would he turn on me like this? We weren't best friends, but I thought we were becoming closer.

"Axel!" I screamed. His name left my lips before I had the chance to stop it.

He howled loudly as he dove at me.

I screamed as I threw my hand up, and a tingling sensation ran down my arm to my palm.

Axel was thrown back. He slammed into a tree and fell unconscious on the ground.

I held my hand to my heaving chest as I heard his bones crack.

I got to my feet while trembling. I felt weak but not faint, thankfully. I walked over to him slowly. I stared with my heart in my throat as he changed into his human form, his body breaking as he shifted.

I bent down and placed my hand behind his head only to take my hand away to see blood coating my fingers. I had done it. I had used my powers. Yet, in the process, I had hurt someone. I had hurt my mate. A sick feeling settled in my chest as I placed my hand on his cheek. "I'm so sorry," I whispered to him as my eyes teared up. "Can you hear me, Axel? Please, wake up."

The rustling of bushes caught my attention, as Xavier appeared in his human form.

I paid no attention to the fact that he was naked. All I

could focus on was my panic, regret, and worry that I might have killed Axel.

"Let me carry him. He's fine. I can hear his heartbeat."

I moved away instantly.

Xavier picked Axel up and took off running.

I did my best to keep up with him. Despite my effort, Xavier was soon so far ahead of me, all I could see was his perfect backside. I slowed my pace until I started walking, the tears I'd been trying to hold back running like little rivers from my eyes.

The feeling of the sun's rays on my skin shining down through the little openings in the canopy of tree leaves above wasn't filling me with happiness like it typically did. I leaned my head back and screamed as loud as I could, and like before, an unseen force left my body to blow the canopy of trees above me back.

I placed my hands on my head as I now stared at the sky above. I looked back down to see Natalie watching me and I rapidly wiped at my tears.

She walked over to me, a look of pity on her face.

We said nothing as we stared at each other for a moment.

"Come on," she urged after a while.

We ambled back to the house in silence.

Axel

I had no idea Ruby was capable of being this annoying. For an hour, she hadn't left my side since I'd woken up. I was only out for about thirty minutes. Since it was 4:45 pm and no wolf would be able to shift after 6 pm, I was able to heal most of my broken bones on my own.

However, I did need little help from Natalie for my cracked skull.

Ruby kept checking on me and asking if I was okay every few minutes. While it was refreshing that she cared so much, it was starting to get on my nerves. She might have gotten a good one in on me, but I'm much harder to kill than she thinks.

"Ruby, I'm fine, okay? Can you stop?" I wasn't a weakling, and I didn't need to be protected or coddled. Not by her, or anyone else for that matter.

Her beautiful face fell.

Seeing the sadness in her eyes was like a punch to my gut. I knew she felt guilty for what happened, but it hadn't been her fault. I reached out and pinched her chin gently as I grinned at her.

The edges of her mouth twitched with a little smile. "Okay, I hear you," she conceded with both hands up in mock surrender.

I knew she'd still be keeping an eye on me though.

"There was a charge in the air," Natalie declared.

I turned to look at her.

She sat perched on the arm of the chair Xavier was sitting on. "The moment Ruby used her power, I could feel it." She shook her head as she pinched the bridge of her nose. "If I hadn't known it was her, I wouldn't have been able to track it. It was like feeling an earthquake. You can feel it, but you can't pinpoint its origin."

"Do you think other creatures will be able to sense her powers?" Mathieu asked.

Natalie shrugged. "I don't know. All of them can sense magic. That includes Enchanteds, witches, and demons. I'm only guessing here, but it would make sense if others can sense her powers since I can now feel it without trying to. It wasn't like that before."

I pressed a finger to my temple, where my previously pounding headache was slowly fading. I glanced over at Ruby.

She'd been observing me before looking away. "It wasn't heat, like it was before," she explained. "With the vampire, it was fire. This time, like with Randoll, it was this..." She looked around as she searched for the right words. "It was energy. I could feel it flowing through my body and in the things around me, the earth, and trees. When I used it on Axel, I felt it coalescing throughout my body and pushing outwards through my arm to attack him."

"So, you can harness the energy in living things then?" Xavier asked. "If you could feel the energy within yourself and use it defensively."

Ruby shrugged. "Maybe, I don't know." She turned to me, her brows furrowing.

I sighed, as I knew what was coming.

"What the hell were you even thinking?" Ruby asked. "I could have killed you!"

"But you didn't, and it worked, didn't it?" I pointed out.

"You could have died," she articulated slowly. "I believed you. I thought something was wrong with you. Never do that again!"

I shrugged as I sighed and placed my elbows on my knees. "I had to make it believable. Your scent is stronger now as well," I added. "We need to do something about that. At this point, even with the barrier around us, vampires and were-wolves *will* be able to smell her."

"We don't have a witch that can create a masking potion," Mathieu pointed out.

"Right," I acknowledged as I leaned back. "I'll have to make a call then. Tomorrow I'll have to go get it, but I won't be able to return right away. In the meantime, Ruby, there is an underground room built on this house, a bunker. You'll have to stay there in order to minimize your scent getting out."

Frowning, she mumbled under her breath, "Great… Sure."

"Less than ideal, I know, but it's just until I get back," I added.

She nodded. "There is something else," Ruby revealed as she faced the others. "I had a vision."

Xavier leaned forward. "When?"

"Today… this morning, that is. There was a white wolf, black smoke, and a giant cobra, and I saw little else. Every time I have this vision, it always ends with the cobra eating me."

"How long have you been having this vision?" Mathieu inquired, concern evident in his voice.

"A while," she replied as she glanced back and forth between Xavier and me.

I noticed we were both shooting her the same angry look.

"I didn't want to say anything. Plus, as weird as it is, massive cobras like that don't even exist for me to be scared of, right?" No one answered, and her face fell. "Wait, they do?"

"Was the wolf a normal wolf or a werewolf?" Mathieu probed further.

"Ahh, I think it was a werewolf. It looked too big to be a regular wolf."

Mathieu hummed thoughtfully. "There are no white werewolves in existence. According to myth, the first of our kind, the purest of all werewolves, was white. No one has ever actually seen a white werewolf, though. "

Ruby made a face. "Well, I think a white werewolf would be pretty awesome-looking and probably less frightening. I'm not trying to call you guys scary, but in all honesty, you are."

Mathieu nodded in agreement. "Our final form is meant to be scary. The first of our kind was said to be white, angelically beautiful because he had our goddess's affection. He was her first creation. The stories say he became tainted by darkness, corrupted. He lost his white fur and transformed yet again into a hideous beast that walked on two feet."

Ruby listened attentively with an obvious fascination.

Her interest made me remember when I had first heard this story. "That's why we have two forms. The first is of a normal, albeit unusually large wolf and the last, that of a bipedal beast, a hybrid of both man and animal. It also explains why changing to our final form is difficult to achieve for most wolves. You're at risk of losing yourself to the animal and remaining in that form."

"Okay, I see," Ruby replied. "Well, that is both tragic and

fascinating. Tragic in that you all have to suffer through it but fascinating that it's even possible."

I snorted. "You wouldn't think it's fascinating in the least, if you'd experienced it," I told her.

"Until you get used to it," Xavier added.

Without warning, Natalie rose to her feet abruptly.

So did Xavier and I as soon as we noticed how the color of her eyes had already shifted to white.

Natalie's head kept moving from side to side as if she was watching something.

Xavier and I shared a look before glancing over at Ruby to make sure she was all right.

Ruby appeared fine, though clearly, she shared our concern for Natalie as she and Mathieu stood as well.

We all knew by now that Natalie's visions rarely brought good news.

"No, no, no," Natalie repeated while swaying a little. She lost her balance and rocked backward as if to fall but caught herself. She reached up to hold her forehead. When she looked up at us after a moment, her eyes had once again resumed their normal shade of blue.

"What's coming?" Mathieu questioned her.

I clenched my jaw. I'd been right to take the risk and come here after all. I had hoped this wouldn't happen, that an attack wouldn't come, but I wasn't surprised something was going to happen.

"They're coming," she whispered to him as her glossy eyes drifted to Ruby. "The humans are coming for her."

5

RUBY

$\mathcal{I}$ wished I could vanish. I wished one of my powers, or even my only power, was the ability to teleport to anywhere I wanted. Better yet, I just wished I were normal.

I didn't want to wish I had never known about werewolves because then I would never have met Xavier, Natalie, and Axel. Not knowing about werewolves would've meant I wouldn't have known about vampires and their plans of world domination. Alone in life with no one to help me, no doubt I would have lost my life the first night the vampires attacked.

I'd been badass enough to look after myself in general, but not when fighting a supernatural being—a vampire. I still had nightmares about the vampire that fed on me. I sighed as I closed my eyes.

Who was I even kidding? If I were being honest, I wasn't quite as much of a badass as I liked to think. I hadn't been able to protect myself against those sick bastards the night I found out Xavier wasn't human. *Xavier* had saved me from whatever sick plans those motherfuckers had in mind for me that night. The world I'd fallen into had its good and bad bits, so taking away one bad thing might result in taking away something I didn't want to lose.

Natalie's words echoed in my head for a moment before I sat down stiffly. *The humans are coming for me.* "There is a full moon," I whispered. I gazed up at the others with wide eyes. "There's a full moon tonight. You guys will be defenseless. We have to leave. We all have to leave now, before nightfall!"

"Ruby," Axel spoke.

Without further hesitation, I jumped to my feet. I wouldn't have the annihilation of this pack or any pack on my hands. "Then I'll leave! I can't let this happen because of me! If I'm not here, the humans will move on," I added.

"Even though we won't be able to shift," Xavier attempted to reason with me. "We're still stronger than any human. Remember that, Ruby. No one can leave right now. It's a full moon tonight, yes. So we know we'll be more at risk out there than being here on the grounds."

I turned my back to them and walked away. I had all this power. Yet, instead of solving my problems, it was only creating more pain and worry. If only we'd been able to find out who I truly was from the start, then maybe I would have learned about my powers and how to control them. Then I'd be an asset in this fight against the vampires, instead being seen as a threat by every side. The vampires hunted me out of fear now, instead of just food, while werewolves and humans alike were just trying to capture me.

Olcan probably wanted to dissect me at this point, and it was highly likely what the humans wanted to do to me too.

"She's not wrong," Axel unexpectedly acknowledged.

I turned around to look at him.

"I have the number for the warlock," he went on. "I can call him and ask him for help. We can't let them get their hands on Ruby, and you all know that. She does need to leave," Axel affirmed.

"Are we seriously back to this right now, Axel?" Xavier asked him in disgust. "We talked about this. It's a no to using black magic."

I frowned unhappily. This wasn't Xavier's decision to make.

"We're not asking that warlock for help, Axel," Xavier argued. "We can handle some humans on our own, whether there is a full moon or not."

Axel shook his head. "You're being naïve, Xavier, and you're underestimating humans. Something that I'm expected to do, not you."

Xavier said nothing as his face hardened.

"Right now, we have no choice," Axel continued. "They're coming for her. We can't let them get to her before we know what she is, or before we know why a barrier was placed in her mind and what's behind it. If you have another idea of how to save her right now, let me hear it."

"And what if you take her to the warlock and the price is too high?" Xavier retorted. "Won't we have to find another way then? So, we can think of another way together now."

Axel rubbed at his forehead with evident frustration. "Xavier, we can't bypass something that might work because we're stuck on what-ifs. If we go to the warlock and the price is too high, we will leave and find another way. If we go to the warlock and it can be done, we would have saved ourselves a lot of time and trouble."

Xavier shook his head. "Axel, I don't think—"

"We're running out of time!" Axel interjected. "She is growing stronger. Her powers are growing stronger. Eventually, the slightest thing might trigger her. She might kill herself and us."

"This is my choice to make!" I yelled.

All eyes turned to me.

"This is my choice to make." I lowered my voice as I sighed. "I understand that there might be a price, Xavier. However, ignoring a viable option simply because we don't know what that price is, or if it can be paid or not, is foolish." I pointed to Natalie. "Nat said they're coming, and we're here bickering. I want to go to the warlock."

Axel nodded.

I continued, "But I'm not leaving now, not if everyone is staying."

Axel frowned. "What?"

"I ran once before, and I won't do it again. It's because of me that the humans are coming for us. My powers might be unstable right now, but if they attack us, I can help. I know I can, and I need you all to trust me on that. I'm the one person who can protect us all… sure, I could kill us all too, but that's not the point." I exhaled heavily through my nostrils. "Just put me in front of everyone, and I'll protect us."

Axel scratched at his jaw as he scrunched his face. "That plan might work, Ruby, but that's not enough. Plus, you can't guarantee you won't lose control. Okay, we need to think about this without arguing. We're going in circles, and we're wasting time."

"Okay," Xavier replied. "If you're not here, Ruby, they will attack anyways. So it's better if you leave, I agree with that.

You're the one they want, so all we can do is defend ourselves the way we would if you were here to be protected. Hopefully, when they realize you aren't here, they'll leave to find you. You staying and hoping your powers make an appearance isn't a plan at all. It's a gamble. If that fails to pay off, we're all in trouble in addition to them getting you."

"The entire pack can't leave," Mathieu finally spoke up. "It's almost nightfall, and the vampires will be hunting. We can fight humans but not vampires. The pack has to stay, but you, Ruby, you have to leave."

With his input, the decision was made.

"How long before they arrive?" Axel asked Natalie, who had been quiet this whole time.

I felt surprised when she didn't have anything to say.

"I saw them arriving at night." She nodded. "And we only have two hours tops of sunlight. I would say they are coming soon."

"I wonder how they found us?" Mathieu mumbled to himself before turning to me. "Our pack doesn't have another safe house, none with warding as strong as here that is."

Axel snapped his fingers suddenly. "Speaking of warding, I need to check on ours." He removed his phone from his pocket, dialed a number, and held it to his ear. The longer the phone rang, the more his brows knitted. The call went unanswered and he hissed as he redialed. "Something is wrong. She's not answering." He peered down at the phone. "The witch that did the warding spells isn't answering." He turned to Natalie. "Can you check if the warding is still strong? Her magic is tied into it. If she's okay, the warding should hold, but if not…"

Natalie stepped forward. "Wardings aren't my thing. I can check if I still feel its energy, but that's all. If it's down, we'll lose one of the greatest advantages we have."

"Check if it's stable." Axel turned to Xavier. "Whether it's stable or not, we have a fight to prepare for."

Ruby

Xavier entered the room with a backpack I had grown sick of seeing. Seeing it make an appearance meant I'd be running for my own protection once more.

He placed it on the ground by the door and walked over to me. "Are you ready?"

I shook my head. "No. I don't like the idea of leaving you behind, Xavier."

"I don't like it either, but you have to. Dad and I need to stay here to help the others, so you have to go with Axel and Natalie." He held my cheeks in his hands.

I bent my head to snuggle further into his hands.

He continued, "Since Natalie said the warding is still there but weak, something must have happened to the witch."

Knowing now what that witch and her coven meant to Axel, I could only imagine how angry he must have been. "Yeah, I know. Is Axel still unable to get through to her?"

Xavier shook his head.

I sighed. "Okay." I listened to the commotion outside the room's door. Some of the wolves that had been sleeping outside were moved inside the house. Warrior wolves would stay outside to be positioned around the house and within the woods. Mathieu had given the pack a choice—stay and fight or leave and fend for themselves. Anyone that left would be allowed to return in the future. A few wolves chose to go, and I didn't blame them. Something was wrong with the warding. Even without the humans attacking, it would only be a matter of time before vampires sniffed us out, especially with my scent mixed in with the cocktail.

With all that was happening, I knew the pack would only hate me more. "I'm so sorry for all of this," I whispered.

Xavier pinched my chin. He tipped my face back for me to look at him.

I closed my eyes and shook my head. "Don't try to tell me I shouldn't be sorry. You and I both know we were found because of me."

"We were found because someone betrayed us and told the humans. That's not on you," he replied. "We have nowhere else to go from here, so this is where we have to make a stand and fight. The warding is down, but we should fight here tonight rather than run and end up defenseless against vampires on a full moon. If your powers can indeed be helpful, Ruby, and I think they can, you have to learn to control them." He shook his head. "The warlock will help, and whatever happens here tonight, you'll be able to avenge it."

I stepped away from him. "Stop talking as if you're going to die tonight."

He sighed. "Ruby—"

"Shut up, Xavier!"

"Okay," he said softly and held his hand out to me. "Come here."

I went back to him without hesitation.

He kissed the top of my head. "I wish I could come with you, but as much as I hate to admit this, I know Axel will look out for you. And Natalie as well."

I looked up at him. I knew Axel would protect me, but I chose not to say anything. I doubted Xavier wanted to hear my thoughts about Axel and his ability to protect me. Both men had been civil for the most part, and their hatred for each other wasn't so stifling anymore. Axel and Xavier weren't on the road to becoming best friends, but I loved that they were getting along for the most part.

We all had no room to think about what would become of our three-way mate bond right now. Once this was all over, we'd have to figure it out. I didn't want to think about whom I would have to reject or who would reject me.

At first, I had thought Axel would be the one to reject me. Now… I wasn't so sure.

I reached up and ran my hand through Xavier's hair. "Be careful, okay?" I tipped up on my toes and kissed him.

He instantly snaked his hands around me and crushed me to his body.

"Or I'm going to be pissed," I whispered against his lips when I pulled away. "And you don't want me to get pissed."

He smirked down at me. "So you think you can take me now, huh? Is that it?"

I poked a finger against his chest. "I know I can."

He looked thoughtful for a moment. "Yeah, I think you could." He kissed my forehead. "I'll come and find you soon, okay?"

We pulled away from each other.

Xavier went over to the door and grabbed my bag.

We made our way downstairs together and I tried not to seem cowardly by keeping my gaze down to avoid looking anyone in the eyes. I stared ahead with my spine straight, and my head held high. I knew what they all thought of me, but I wouldn't allow them to think I was a sucker.

The nasty looks were like hot metal on my skin, but I endured it and kept walking. The moment we stepped outside, Xavier quickly grabbed my hand, and the wolves positioned outside stopped what they were doing. It took a moment for me to realize what was happening when I heard the speeding car, and then it appeared.

It skidded to a halt. Three men from the pack that had chosen to leave the pack, jumped out.

"They've blocked us in!" one of them yelled.

Xavier released my arm as Axel moved up to my other side.

"Who?" Xavier asked as he stepped forward. "What happened?"

Another car returned as well with three other men. "The humans created a blockade at our exit. We're trapped," the man that had first spoken replied.

"The vision changed," Natalie stated from behind me.

I turned to look at her.

Her brows furrowed. "The vision I saw was during the night…" She stared at me. "It's changed."

Randoll walked up to Xavier, his shirtless chest glistening with sweat. "I'll take two others and check the woods. Maybe there is a path we can take out of here to avoid them."

Xavier clenched his jaw. "The women and children can't leave tonight. They'll be picked off first if vamps attack us. Plus, a large pack of wolves traveling together will be like a buffet that vamps will smell from miles away." He then looked over at me. "Find a pathway quickly."

Randoll nodded, pointed at two men, and they all took off into the woods.

Xavier turned to me and led me back inside the house. "If there is a path, you guys need to take it and get out of here," Xavier glanced at Axel. "Don't leave her side." He turned and walked away.

"Xavier!" I called.

He kept moving away as he called back to me, "I'll be right back."

I turned to look at Natalie.

Her face was still scrunched up, no doubt annoyed that her vision had changed. "We only have an hour left before sundown. If we're to leave, it has to be now," she said.

Axel nodded. "It's best if Randoll checks the forest first before we make a run for it. If they've blocked our exit, they might have men in the woods right now, because the only option we have now is to escape through the woods."

I took a deep breath and then another. "Okay, maybe I should go down to that bunker you were talking about earlier. Is it well hidden? Humans can't smell me, right? Everyone can tell them I'm not here, and we will see if they'll leave."

Natalie puckered her mouth in thought. "We could do that, yes, unless they whip out dogs to track your scent."

I sighed. For every solution, I was met with a "try again." I'd really like to get my hands on whoever informed on us. I looked around at the people all gathered around, some still staring at me while others were busy having their own conversations.

A loud boom echoed through the woods, and the house fell silent.

Axel, Natalie, and I exchanged a look.

I dashed towards the door as another boom sounded, this time closer.

Once outside, we ran into Xavier and four other men. "What is that?" I asked.

"Bomb," Xavier replied as his eyes changed to black. "It's after six. We can't shift."

Axel grabbed my hand to tug me back.

I pulled away. The time for escaping had passed... the only remaining option seemed to be that we face these people. I hoped a fight didn't have to happen. I closed my eyes and listened to my heartbeat.

I tried to focus on the fear and panic I was feeling and decided to use them to call on the power within me.

"Ruby, don't," Natalie warned.

My eyes popped open. "I have to try," I replied through clenched teeth.

Just then, a loud voice boomed through the trees, *"We don't want to fight! We're only here for the girl!"*

I clenched my fists.

Randoll stepped out of the woods while carrying an unconscious wolf. Two humans in black army gear had guns aimed at Randoll, who had blood running down his face from a wound on his forehead.

"Your friend isn't dead! He tried to attack us and was shot with a tranquilizer. We don't want to fight. We only wish to talk!"

Behind Randoll, two more humans appeared, their guns pointed at the other wolf Randoll had taken with him.

Then from behind them, a man stepped out with a loudspeaker in hand. His chestnut blonde hair was cut low, and unlike the other men that were dressed for war, he was wearing a black skin-tight t-shirt. He stopped walking, and so did the others as his dark blue eyes fell on me instantly. He looked me up and down.

I returned the gesture to him.

Clearly, he was the one in charge here. He looked at Xavier and motioned with his hand to the man in Randoll's arms. "Your friend will be fine. He just needs to sleep off the drugs." His hand fell to his side. "We apologize for—"

"Cut the shit and get to the point," Axel cut him off. "What do you want?"

The man's eyes fell on me once more, and the corner of his mouth arched with a smile. "We want to talk to the alpha." His lips stretched into a genuine smile, one mixed with almost excitement. "Hello, Ruby, our little vampire slayer. It's nice to finally meet you."

6

RUBY

"We're an elite fighting group created to hunt vampires," General Presley explained. "After the first week, the first vampire wave, the government created the P.E.A, the Paranormal Eradication Agency. Every member has been selected from multiple government agencies based on their skill sets. We all possess skills that will put us at an advantage above the average human."

"So, you're a vampire hunter, basically?" Natalie asked.

Presley nodded. His eyes wandered to me.

I stared back at him with a blank expression.

Mathieu had invited him in. So here we were, a happy bunch just sitting in the living room, having a chat. The fight that we had expected to happen... didn't. While I was pleased that lives would not be lost tonight, this man—General Presley—was here for me.

Over my dead body would I be leaving with General Presley, no matter how much he insisted he was on our side.

Axel remained close to me. Xavier stood by his father's

side, but he kept looking my way. He looked just as unhappy as I was about the entire situation.

The way that I saw it, all of this talking was wasting time. General Presley would eventually get to the part where he needed me to go with him. Maybe the fight was only being delayed until then because there was no way in hell I was leaving—not with him, anyways.

"So, you see, my people aren't the ones targeting wolves," Presley directed this comment to Axel, who was making no effort to hide his animosity towards the General and his men. "We're on your side. It's clear for anyone to see...well, obviously only some people know that werewolves have been living alongside us peacefully for who knows how long." He looked back at Mathieu, "If you guys had been killing and targeting humans, someone would have noticed. You don't... you know... eat hu—"

"No," Axel interjected. "We do not eat humans. However, if werewolves were hunting humans, there is absolutely no guarantee you guys would have noticed." Axel smirked. "Vampires aren't the only supernaturals humans need to fear. They are just the only ones on a murdering-slash-world-domination rampage."

As much as I already disliked Presley, Axel's tactic to scare him was a double-edged sword. He was telling Presley that there were more supernaturals out there to scare him, but this had essentially put other supernaturals onto his radar. Something he would no doubt report. Especially after what they'd experienced with the vampires, if and when humans discovered other powerful supernaturals, they would kill them purely out of fear, just as they had done with the werewolves.

"Fair enough," Presley acknowledged quietly as he sent a look to two of his men standing by the door. "My point is, werewolves aren't the threat. Vampires are."

"If only the rest of your people would realize that," Mathieu replied. "You're killing the one species that can truly help with fighting the vampires... the only ones willing to fight, actually. Humans aren't generally well-liked by the supernatural community."

Presley frowned. "I know. Humans can be difficult, stubborn, and untrustworthy at times. We can also be kind, helpful, and persistent. We have our good and bad sides, just like anyone else. You invited a human into your pack, so you must have seen..." He smiled at me as he paused. "...we're not all bad."

"What are you doing here, General Presley?" Mathieu asked bluntly.

"There are no vampires to be hunted here," Axel added defensively.

Axel's protectiveness for me was clear, and it made me blush. We'd come a long way from where things were before. Natalie and Xavier were no longer the only ones that genuinely cared for me.

Presley got to his feet and walked to the window beside the bookshelves, his hands clasped behind his back. He turned to face us after a moment. A new emotion appeared in his eyes, a seriousness that hadn't been there before. He stood straight, his chest and head high. "We need your help." He then turned to me. "We need *your* help, Ruby."

"She can't help you," Xavier replied before I could.

Presley sent a puzzled look Xavier's way in response to his territorial behavior.

I'm certain he was wondering whether Xavier was my boyfriend. What he didn't know - and probably never could've guessed - was that the other one standing by my side was mine as well. My eyes widened at my thoughts. Why was I thinking of Axel as if he was my man? He's my mate, not my man. There was a difference. I rolled my eyes at myself. Now wasn't the time to muddle over my feelings for Axel. I wondered what Presley would think when he found out I wasn't just Xavier's girl but his mate. How would he react to that? Would he freak out at the thought that humans could be mated to wolves?

"What happened to her was an accident. She can't help you when she has no control over her gifts," Xavier added quickly.

"I can't help you," I told him.

He shook his head. "You can. You killed two vampires," Presley insisted.

I clenched my jaws.

"This is true, right?" he asked. "You burned them to death without even touching them."

I shifted my weight from one leg to the other nervously.

Presley stepped forward.

Axel pinned him with a glare.

He stopped abruptly. "What are you?" Presley asked. "Tell me that, at least. If you don't want to help, maybe there might be others in your species that will be willing to. To be honest, we are losing to the vampires. More of them pop up every night. We need help. We need to help each other."

"How would I help?" I asked. "Xavier's right. I can't control my gifts, but even if I wanted to help, how would I?" I swallowed hard before I continued, "There aren't others like me. I'm the only one of my kind. How would I help to stop a global attack by myself?"

Presley didn't seem surprised by what I said.

I had to wonder if he already knew. Did he know everything already about Xavier, Axel, and me as well? No, he couldn't. The only rumor that had gone around about me was that I killed two vampires, not how I did it nor the fact I'm mated to two wolves.

"We have a private facility," he replied. "You'd be taken there, and we'd be able to examine your gifts."

"Examine?" I asked.

Beside me, Axel shook his head vehemently. "He means you'll become a lab rat," Axel seethed.

My arm twitched as I picked up a burst of energy coming from him.

"Why do you need to test her abilities in a lab?" Axel took a step forward. "If you want her help, she'd join your team. She'd use her powers in the field to offer help. How will running tests on her solve anything?"

Presley's brows furrowed.

"There is a better and faster solution," Axel went on. "Get your people to stop hunting werewolves! Here's a history lesson for you. Werewolves were the ones to eradicate vampires before. If you morons let up, we'd be able to do it again. What do you think will happen if you kill the vampires' main rival, huh?"

Presley inhaled deeply, irritation evident in his features as he too, stepped forward. "Thanks for the history lesson, but you said it yourself. She can't control her powers. She'd be taken to a private facility to train. Being on the field with us means she'd have to know *how* to work alongside us. We'd need to know how her gifts work and understand how they can be incorporated with our plans and resources in order to maximize her impact." He unclasped his hands from behind his back. "As for making demands to cease killing were-wolves, I can't do that."

The sensation in my arm grew as Axel clenched his fists. "And why is that?"

"I don't have the authority. I'm in charge of the P.E.A, and that's all. I'm not in a position to make demands. I don't get a say in matters being handled by other departments."

"And we're not in a position to give up one of our own," Axel rejoined with a deep growl in his voice.

"Axel," I warned.

He kept his sharp eyes trained on Presley.

The two men by the door stepped forward.

Natalie stood up from where she had been seated.

They stared at her with narrowed eyes as she blocked their way to Presley before turning to watch Xavier as well, who stepped forward, no doubt in case they attacked Natalie.

"We only need her help and that's all," Presley explained. "I get that you're angry about your people being killed and that you don't trust us, but we're all dying out there. Vampires are killing everyone, and my job is to work on killing them." He raised his hand to point his finger at me. "Behind you stands the only solution I currently have. You say there is only one of her, but are you sure of that? If we're able to test her blood, her genes, maybe we can locate others. We'd stand a chance in this fight with powers like hers on our side. Testing Ruby to see if her powers might be useful shouldn't be a problem. She'll be helping to save lives."

"It shouldn't be a problem?" Axel enunciated slowly, his voice low.

I closed my eyes and grimaced as the tingling in my arm started to change. I raised my hand to wipe away sweat from my forehead and my heartbeat spiked as I realized what was happening. I looked at Mathieu as he stared at me. Then I winced as I heard Axel's deep growl.

His claws had pierced through his fingers.

Presley's eyes widened as Axel's fangs elongated.

Axel's energy, his anger, was affecting me. I stepped back and away from everyone as I gritted my teeth to try and hold back what was building up inside me. Why had Axel's anger affected me? Whatever was happening to me right now wouldn't be a shock wave, and I sent a petrified look Mathieu's way.

"Axel! That's enough! Calm down!" Mathieu thundered.

I jumped as his baritone voice echoed throughout the room.

Axel stepped back and retracted his claws.

The level of dominance Mathieu had used was only making me feel worse. I gazed down at my hands and whimpered as I saw how red they looked. The blue veins at my wrist turned red, and my eyes widened. I was sure that hadn't happened the last time.

"Ruby?" Natalie whispered, "Are you okay?" She took a step towards me.

I looked up quickly and stepped back as I held both my hands on my chest. "Don't!" I cried.

Natalie froze.

I looked directly at Axel. "Stay back, all of you."

His fangs vanished and his rage died as his face twisted with concern. He and Xavier shared a look.

I turned to Presley.

He stared at me with shock, fear, and fascination all rolled into one. "What's happening to her?" He hesitated. "Is she losing control?"

"Trust me," I answered through clenched teeth, "you better pray I'm not. I suggest you all stop the fucking arguing. Going or staying is my decision!"

The temperature in the room spiked.

Axel stepped towards me cautiously. "Come with me, Ruby." He held his hand out towards the door.

I swallowed, suddenly feeling parched. I moved towards Axel, maintaining a safe distance from him as I went by him to go through the door. Now would be the worst possible time for me to have a meltdown. I sent an apologetic look to Xavier.

Axel closed the door behind us. "Let's take a breather, okay?"

We made our way up through the house.

It took a few minutes, but I managed to get my powers back under control.

Axel remained by my side in silence as we stood on the second floor's balcony. The full moon hanging low above us, coupled with the cool night's wind, created the perfect environment for me to calm down.

Ever since I met Xavier and started to become comfortable with his pack, I realized I had a deep love for nature. Now that one of my powers was the ability to detect and maybe use the energy in things around me, my bond with the earth had only grown stronger.

As Axel and I headed back downstairs, I wondered if this ability was evolving. At first, I had been able to sense the energy within the earth, trees, and another person, like I had while Axel was chasing me. However, it didn't affect me directly. Yet, just now, Axel's energy caused a physical reaction in me. It was as if my powers had been awakened by his energy.

I was able to use my own energy as a weapon when I forced it from my body. What if I was able to absorb and use energy from the earth, trees, flowers, animals...even people?

The house was alive with whispers and hushed conversations. No doubt, everyone was on edge since there were human men with guns casually hanging around.

Axel and I walked into the living room, and everyone fell silent. They glared at me, and I ground my teeth as I stood my ground.

A few people finally looked away as they continued with their conversations.

"I'm truly loved around here," I mumbled sarcastically to Axel.

When he didn't reply, I looked at him to find him staring daggers at a group of men whispering among themselves.

I frowned as I bumped his arm with mine. "Hey, is everything o…"

He walked off before I was able to finish my sentence. "Say it again!" he thundered to the men.

The room fell silent again.

The men stood up straight as Axel stood in front of them.

I looked around, confused about what was happening until I realized what Axel had said. Those men must have been talking about me.

"You heard what we said, so we don't need to repeat ourselves," one man said as he crossed his arms over his chest.

Axel stepped forward and this time when he spoke, his voice was low and somehow more intimidating than when he had yelled, "Say it again."

Another man snorted, as he looked Axel up and down. "You don't belong here. Stop walking around here like you're the alpha for us. You should leave and take that *thing* with you too."

"What the fuck did you just call me?" I yelled. A hand came down on my shoulder. I whipped around, ready to tear the person a new asshole for touching me and found Xavier looking down at me. I calmed instantly.

His eyes darted away from mine, as they turned black. He stepped around me and into the room.

Several people stepped out of his way.

I wasn't feeling his energy, but I didn't need to with the clear dominance within his walk. "A thing...is that what she is?" he asked slowly and calmly, his voice dangerously low.

The wolves that had been whispering didn't answer.

"I asked a question… is that what Ruby is? A thing? Aren't we all considered 'things' to humans and some other super-naturals? Hmm? No one here has the right to judge Ruby for being different. A werewolf born alone without a pack or knowledge of what they were would be exactly like she is now. Be thankful that you have a pack around you and show some compassion for the fact that she doesn't." His shoulders rose and fell as he inhaled deeply. "Apologize to your Luna," he ordered. "Apologize!"

The men glared at me, their jaws tightly clenched. All mumbled an apology.

Xavier turned around to face me as Natalie, Mathieu and General Presley entered the room.

"Someone here betrayed us," Natalie announced.

Now, the room was overtaken with whispers.

Axel and Xavier walked back over to stand beside me.

Natalie went on, "The humans found us because they were told about our location."

"A mind link will be done tonight to find who this traitor is," Mathieu added. "These are dark, confusing times, but we're the Blackmoon Pack. We remain strong through our reliance on each other and our loyalty to the pack. We have to be able to count on one another and trust each other. If we can't stand together as one, we will fall." He glanced over at General Presley. "Our pack might have been attacked tonight on a full moon because someone here betrayed our location and put everyone at risk." Now he gazed at the men in the room. "I know some of you recently started to question whether I have been acting in the best interest of the pack. Rest assured, the pack's safety is my number one priority, and every decision I have made has been with the pack's security in mind. Yes, Ruby has the power to kill vampires, which means she has a power that none of the rest of us do. Her power will help to save us all. I know tensions are high right now, but Ruby is one of us. She deserves our support and respect. Whoever was angry enough to reveal our location, step forward now, and you will not be punished."

I'd never been lucky enough to hear Mathieu speak to his people, but the sincerity, respect, and love in his voice explained why he was so loved and had one of the largest packs. I felt a tug on my heart as I stared at Mathieu, but then I caught Presley staring at me. I narrowed my eyes at him.

Presley looked away.

No one stepped forward.

Mathieu nodded to Natalie to proceed with the mind link.

Presley stepped back. No doubt, he wanted to see what was about to happen but from a safer distance.

I was surprised Mathieu was allowing him to see this. Even so, I dismissed him from my mind because I was too curious about what was about to happen. I'd never seen Natalie do a mind link on the entire pack.

She rolled her shoulders and exhaled as she closed her eyes.

Everyone in the room did the same. The house, crammed top to bottom with wolves, was silent enough to hear a pin drop.

When Natalie reopened her eyes, they were as white as snow. Everyone else's eyes opened, but they remained still as Natalie's eyes started blinking rapidly. It went on like that for a few minutes. Suddenly, she took a deep breath and staggered slightly.

In a blink, Xavier was there to support her.

Around the room, many people began groaning and pressing their fingers into their temples.

I knew how they felt. Mind links could be draining and even painful at times. Having someone rummage around your thoughts and memory was as unpleasant as it sounded.

"Where is she?" Natalie yelled, the tips of her ears turning red, as she grew angry. "Where is she?"

A deep growl echoed through the room and several people from the center of the crowd were backing away.

Suddenly, from out of nowhere, a wolf flew through the air, knocking others over in the process. It charged me at full speed with sharp white canines bared.

Everything happened so quickly I could barely process it. As Mathieu grabbed me and pulled me behind him, a loud pop echoed through the room.

The wolf fell to the ground, motionless.

All eyes turned to Presley, who had his handgun raised. "It is only a tranquilizer," he reassured us as he placed the gun back into his holster.

I stepped around Mathieu to see the wolf. I watched as the unconscious wolf began to shift into Anna. Although there were plenty of people in the pack that I knew would love to see me disappear for good, I wasn't surprised that Xavier's ex-girlfriend was the one who ultimately revealed our location to the humans. She hated me from the very start, and everything that had happened since had done nothing to improve the situation or our relationship.

"Amazing," Presley remarked, clearly fascinated.

Randoll stepped forward and covered Anna's naked body with his jacket.

"Lock her up," Xavier told him.

Randoll picked up Anna none too gently and left the room.

I watched Randoll carry her away, and my shoulders fell dejectedly. Even though she was a world-class asshole, I felt terrible. To be clear, I didn't feel bad because she was a traitorous bitch. I felt bad because I knew she placed the entire pack at risk as a result of her hatred towards me. Once again, my presence had a negative impact on the pack. I sighed. Logically, I knew it wasn't my fault, but I couldn't help but feel responsible.

Mathieu placed his hand on my shoulder. "You need to come with me."

I leaned my head back somewhat to look up at him. I looked at Xavier and Axel, who were watching me.

Axel looked as concerned as I was about Mathieu randomly wanting to speak to me, while Xavier looked almost apologetic.

"Why?" I asked.

Mathieu removed his hand from my shoulder and gave me a stern look before walking away.

I felt like I was in trouble. I also knew whatever Mathieu had to say to me wouldn't be to my liking.

If I was truly a part of the Blackmoon Pack now, he was my alpha too. I followed behind him obediently as my heart hammered in my chest.

7

MATHIEU

J took Ruby to the small office I'd created for myself. She walked in ahead of me and I closed the door behind before crossing the room to my makeshift bar.

Ruby paced as she quickly pulled her hair into a ponytail.

I poured her a glass of brandy.

She hesitated as I handed the glass to her, her green eyes looking up at me with more pain than any woman her age should have. Her fingers wrapped around the glass slowly as she stared into the glass almost thoughtfully before putting it to her lips. She took a sip and then downed it all in one gulp. She shook her head and gave the glass back to me before sitting down.

I smiled at her as I took the glass back. From the moment I met her, Ruby had impressed me with her courage. She had a level of bravery uncommon not only among humans, but supernaturals as well. Despite the non-stop pressure and stress she'd been under since the fateful day she'd discovered who Xavier *really* was, she still held her ground. Of course, she had her understandable moments of fear and doubt, but she never let it get the better of her. Most people would have folded by now.

Ruby was going through a strange transformation without any information as to why it was happening or how it would progress. I need only imagine being a young transitioning werewolf all alone and without a pack to get a bitter taste of the pain she must be feeling. Xavier had been spot on with that reference.

Xavier cared for her deeply, and I could tell by watching them when they were together, the feelings were mutual for her. I didn't know how strong the physical feelings of the mate bond were for her, but the chemistry and affection between them was obvious. They might have gotten started on the wrong foot, but they were headed in the right direction now.

What Xavier didn't know was that his mother and I hadn't gotten along in the beginning either. Our mate bond had triggered upon seeing each other, but we had to learn to live with one another. Little flaws we both initially found annoying about one another eventually became unimportant as our love grew, and two years after the day we met, Xavier was born.

Xavier and Ruby reminded me of his mother and myself. Despite all that had happened and was happening, I'd been happy Ruby was mated to Xavier. Putting all the strangeness of a three-way interspecies mating bond aside, she was more than a human. She would strengthen us—this pack would be the first to evolve. I had skeptical thoughts about her in the beginning, but by now I knew Xavier had found himself a worthy mate.

Now, if we could just deal with the vampire threat, then we finally could get back to our lives. Yet, even if we did manage to vanquish the vamps for good, I knew the world wouldn't be the same after this. It would take time for the world to recover.

"How are you feeling?" I asked her.

She sighed deeply. "My powers weren't triggered by what just happened, if that's what you're worried about."

"But they activated when Axel was arguing with General Presley?"

She nodded.

I'd noticed how close she'd been getting to Axel, and Xavier had too. What was surprising to me was that both Xavier and Axel didn't appear to have that burning flame of hatred between them anymore. It had happened so gradually, I doubt either of them had noticed. Had Ruby ended years of bad blood between our packs by being with them both?

At first, I thought Axel would surely reject her. Now, I knew he wouldn't. How a relationship would play out between all three of them, I couldn't begin to guess.

Ruby pinched the bridge of her nose. "Anna hates me so much that she risked everyone else's life."

"Anna hates everyone," I replied as I leaned on the edge of my desk. "She's always been a bitter girl. I think the only person she's ever cared about was Xavier."

Her hand fell away from her face as she stared at me. "He has that effect on people. It's impossible to dislike him for long. I should know. I certainly tried." She gave me a wry smile.

"The Xavier Effect seems to be working on Axel as well.

75

He's another person that doesn't tend to play nice with others."

A blush crept onto her cheeks. "Going on the run together and being forced to work together in order to survive has caused them to look past the issues they had in the past."

"Or it's your doing?" I postulated.

She frowned.

"Axel could only fight the mate bond for so long," I added. "And so could you. Xavier and Axel are mated to you and not each other, but their shared love for you has changed them... and for the better."

She looked away, but her blush deepened. "Thank you for what you said back there," she replied after a moment, changing the subject.

My lips parted and then closed once more. She wouldn't feel so positively towards me when I told her the reason I wanted to talk to her. "You're my son's mate, the future Luna for this pack. You don't need to thank me. But..." I crossed my arms over my chest. "I need you to go with General Presley."

She got up instantly, her eyes wide with surprise. "What?"

"Ruby..."

She shook her head vehemently. "No, Mathieu. How could you say that? I don't care if he claims to be on our side. They will do to me what Olcan wanted to do."

"Olcan wanted to kill you, Ruby," I replied calmly. "Presley needs you. There is a difference."

"You're too trusting," she muttered.

I chuckled. "I trusted you, didn't I?" I asked pointedly.

She sighed as she moved away. She placed her palms flat

against the wall and began pushing herself back and forth as if she was doing push-ups. Her hands fell to her side after a moment. She turned to look directly at me, her eyes glossy and filled with panic, though she kept a straight face otherwise.

"There is no other way, Ruby," I explained. "I would not say this to you if I felt like General Presley would hurt you. Besides..." I glanced over to the open window and the moon shining bright in the sky. "He's desperate. We've been protected here and have no idea how bad things have gotten out there." I looked back at her and stood up. "He came here for you. While things are calm now, it might not stay that way for much longer because he won't leave without you. In the end, if they can help you with honing your powers, maybe you'll be able to break through that barrier in your mind yourself."

"Plus, if I lose control, it's better I hurt them than you guys," she said jokingly. The sadness returned to her eyes as she hung her head. "I don't want to go with him, Mathieu. You might not have a bad feeling about this, but I do."

"Let me put it this way. He has the firepower to kill us all right now. His men are out there in the forest waiting. We'd still kill many of his men if it came to a fight, but the grim reality is there is a full moon. You know what that means. I'm not saying to trust him. I'm saying to trust me. You are indeed changing and changing into something strong... dangerous. Eventually, no one will be able to hurt you. Not vampires, not Olcan and the Council, nor even General Presley."

"What if I'm changing into something that will hurt you guys too?"

I walked over to her and placed both hands on her shoulder. "You're mated to one of us. We're your people. Focus on finding out what your powers are and how to control them. We can find out what you are later on down the line, and the same goes for your memories. We have to work with what we have at the moment. Okay?"

She swallowed hard and nodded. "Ok. I'll go."

Of course, it would be useful to understand how she knew Lovette and had access to the rest of her memories. Yet, if those memories didn't somehow show her what she was and how to control her powers, we would have just wasted a lot of time.

Her powers were growing stronger by the day, and that was what we need to focus on right now. If humans were coming to us for help, the situation out there must be dire. We would work with General Presley. By cooperating, hopefully we would build trust with the humans. In time, perhaps they would allow us to help them hunt our common enemy.

"I'll come with you," Ruby announced as we entered the room.

Presley released a sigh as if he had been holding his breath. "Good," he replied. "Thank you."

"Don't thank me yet. I'll leave with you, but I'm not leaving without Axel and Xavier."

I smiled and shook my head. I should have known she'd have her own terms.

Presley shook his head. "I'm afraid that won't be possible. My orders are to take you back and only you. My team doesn't hunt werewolves, but the people that hired me don't like anything supernatural right now. Except for you, of course," he added the last bit quickly.

Ruby stepped forward to stand inches away from him. "The people that hired you are killing the wrong supernaturals. They're idiots. They are killing the ones that can help them. This world belongs to us, too. The Blackmoon Pack has been protecting humans for generations." She pointed to Axel and Xavier. "I leave with them, or I don't leave at all." Her hands fell to her sides, and her voice was low when she next spoke, "Since you said you won't be leaving here without me, I will defend my family if you attack us. Understand this: I'm not affected by the full moon. Do you really want to risk pissing me off, General Presley?" She leaned forward and whispered, "I don't have any control, remember?" She stepped back and smiled widely, practically daring General Presley to cross her.

I glanced over at Xavier and Axel, unsurprised to see them gazing at Ruby with proud expressions on their faces. Several wolves were looking on with shocked expressions. I smiled.

"Okay," Presley replied after a moment. "Let's go." He paused to look at me.

I nodded as he walked out of the room.

Ruby glanced over at me as if asking if she had done well.

I nodded approvingly and winked at her.

"When did you become such a badass?" Xavier teased as he walked up behind her. He kissed the top of her head before placing his hand on my shoulder. "We'll be back soon."

I placed my hand on his shoulder and squeezed. "You have no other choice but to come back." I pulled him in for a hug, a rare action, but I needed to hold my son. While remaining positive was important, I knew there was no guarantee this would end well for all of us.

Ruby glanced at Axel and smiled before winking at me.
He smirked and left the room.

"Take care of each other," I advised as I released Xavier.
He took Ruby's hand into his.

"We will," the couple replied in unison.

Ruby

*J*t took an hour for us to get to a town. I wasn't
ready for what we saw.

I'd always been a fan of apocalyptic movies. There had
always been something about a city in ruin with the heroes
and heroines fighting to survive that seemed entertaining to
me. Now, I was a part of something like that, and it wasn't
entertaining at all. It was terrifying.

As we drove through the small town slowly, I looked
from side to side in shock at the destroyed buildings, burnt
cars and rubbish scattered everywhere. We were driving
through what was now a ghost town with not a soul in sight.
Then it hit me—a whiff of the repulsive stench I'd come to
associate with vampires.

I looked over at Xavier on my right and then at Axel on
my left.

Axel was busy staring out his window, his fists clenched.

The world was being destroyed piece by piece. Our car
had to drive up onto the sidewalk because three abandoned
vehicles were poorly parked in the middle of the road. I

gazed around, a little frantic at the loud sound of tires screeching echoed outside.

I caught sight of a dog bolting across the road as the car behind us regained control. I sighed heavily and turned back around. "This is depressing," I said sadly.

"How do you think they feel?" Axel asked as he pointed through his window.

Sure enough, a man and a woman were sprinting, machetes in their hands. Their clothes were shredded. The car's light from behind ours illuminated them. I frowned at the dirt and blood caked to the woman's face as she watched us drive by.

"I can smell them," Axel observed. "It's faint, but I can smell them."

"I've recently come to understand," Presley shared from the front seat. "That vampires have a distinct odor that can be detected by supernaturals. I'm sure it won't surprise you when I tell you we humans have never observed a scent."

"No, humans wouldn't notice anything out of the ordinary. Vampires hunt everything with a bloodstream, yes, but humans are their primary source of nutrients. Mostly because they lack the ability to detect them. The average human wouldn't know a vampire stood right behind them until their fangs pierced the human's neck."

"You speak about us as if we're useless," the driver snapped.

My brows rose as Xavier and I shared a look. Clearly, Axel had hit a nerve.

"I didn't say your kind is useless." Axel exhaled and turned back to his window. "I'm simply stating a fact. I also said the *average* human. Smelling them comes in handy when trying to find them."

"They are everywhere now," Presley explained.

I sat up.

"I don't know what those two were doing out, but they took a big risk," he continued. "You look at this town, and you'd think everyone is just hunkered down indoors for safety, but most of the people are actually either turned or dead. "

Axel spoke again, "I don't think the vampires have thought this through. Yes, humans aren't their only source of food, but it would be stupid to wipe humans off the face of the planet. That's what will happen if they are all dead or turned."

"As plentiful as these vampires are," Presley replied. "It'll be years before they can completely wipe out the human race. Even so, a few days ago, we raided a coven and found sixty humans being kept as a food source."

"Oh," I whispered. "That makes sense then." I kept trying not to imagine the things those people must have gone through. They were being kept as food like cattle. The General's comment triggered a memory from the day I had burned the vampires. I remembered the vampire Rafael had offered to keep me as a pet. According to him, I'd be cared for, and I'd be his food source in exchange. I shuddered. "Those humans you guys found, were they being treated well, or were they in cages and such?" I inquired hesitantly.

"Cages, others were chained up in rooms. Why would you ask if they were being cared for?" Presley responded as he turned to look at me.

"A vampire I met said he'd take me as a pet. Were there

any other humans there, ones that didn't seem like they were being treated too badly?"

Presley shook his head. "No. I doubt vampires know how to care for anything. They're savages."

"Not all of them," Xavier replied.

Presley scoffed. "They are all monsters." He turned around once more to say something else, but as he did so, the car in front of ours exploded.

Our vehicle stopped abruptly, sending me flying forward, but Axel quickly grabbed me.

"What the fuck was that?" Presley yelled.

As I looked up, a cloud of black smoke rose out of the fire.

"What the hell?" Presley said as he too, stared at the smoke as it swirled into the sky and vanished.

A shadow dashed by Axel's door. "That wasn't a vampire," he said.

I spun around, almost falling off the seat as the car behind us exploded as well.

"We need backup now! We have the asset, but we're under attack!" Presley yelled into his phone.

Our driver stepped on the gas. He swung around the burning car and sped up as Presley continued to yell into his phone. "What the hell was that? That wasn't a vampire?"

"I don't know, it was like smoke," Axel replied. "It could have been a demon."

"Just fucking great, now there are demons. Why would it attack us?"

Our car swung violently from left to right, and I hung onto the back of Presley headrest. "It could have been hired by someone to attack your team, or it's doing it on its own accord. Either way, demons aren't to be messed with, so I suggest driving faster."

"I'm going as fast as I can!" the driver yelled as he glanced back at us.

My eyes widened as the smoke appeared before the car. "Watch out!" I shouted.

The driver swung around and stepped on the brakes.

Again, I was thrown forward and was grabbed by Xavier this time.

"Fuck this," the driver hissed as he got out of the car.

"No!" I yelled.

It was too late. He was already outside shooting at the smoke. Of course, the bullets did nothing, as the smoke engulfed him and his body fell to the ground like a sack of potatoes.

Presley growled with rage, like he too, was a werewolf. "All my men are dead, all of them!"

I paused, however, because I could've sworn I glimpsed a face within the smoke.

Xavier reached over and grabbed Presley, who was trying to get out of the car. "Werewolves can't fight smoke, and we're not at full strength yet. You're human, so what can you do? We need to go!"

Presley ignored Xavier as he got out of the car.

Xavier followed and exited the car.

I slid out of the vehicle behind Xavier, and Axel followed.

It had become painfully obvious that we couldn't outrun this thing by driving, so our only option was to make a stand and fight.

I sank my nails into the palms of my hand as I tried to dig deep into myself and harness my power.

"Who are you? What are you?" Presley yelled as he raised his gun. "You just killed innocent men!"

The swirling smoke stilled for a moment.

I frowned.

We all watched as it began to coalesce somewhat.

I suddenly realized something as it charged at Presley. I ran forward and pushed Presley out of the way. "No!" I screamed.

The smoke heading to attack him on the ground—suddenly halted.

Xavier and Axel ran up to me, and I was yanked back by one of them. I shook them off, however, and pointed. "Look."

A man's body was starting to appear as the smoke came together to create a shadow.

My heart was beating so loudly, it hammered in my ears. I looked at the shadow up and down. "It's you," I blurted.

The shadow's head tilted to the side.

"What's going on, Ruby?" Xavier asked.

"It's him—the warlock Axel's witch friend recommended. Axel called him before we left."

The shadow stepped closer to us.

I narrowed my eyes. "You didn't have to kill them." For some reason, I felt like I'd seen this shadow before. I grabbed Axel's arm. "You!"

Xavier stepped in front of me.

I peeped around him as the shadow began to shimmer, and a man, a real man, appeared. He had black eyes, much like a werewolf, and red hair. We watched as he brushed his hands down the sleeve of his long black coat. "Hello, Ruby," he said pleasantly. "Nice to see you again."

I stepped out from behind Xavier.

The warlock's black eyes remained glued to me as I backed away from Axel and Xavier to move further away from him.

Axel held his hand up to the warlock as he took a step forward. "Stop. What's wrong with you? I'm Axel, the one that called you. You didn't need to kill those men."

A gunshot echoed, and the warlock staggered backward as Presley shot him and then again and again. Almost as if someone had pressed a slow motion rewind button, I watched as the bullets pushed themselves back out of his body and the holes in his chest healed. His hand shot out, and smoke engulfed Presley.

"No!" I yelled.

It was too late. Presley fell backward, and his gun fell from his hand.

"Don't worry," the warlock reassured me. "He's only unconscious. After all, you told me not to kill him."

"You bastard!" I screamed.

"Do you know this guy?" Xavier asked.

I turned to him to explain, "This is the guy who was inside my dungeon. The same one who was inside my motel room." My eyes narrowed at the warlock. "Were you the one that saved us when vampires attacked us? I know you've been following us."

The warlock smiled. "As I said, it's nice to see you again, Ruby. Shall we get going?"

8

RUBY

*T*he awkward silence in the car was unbearable, for me at least. I kept my eyes glued to the warlock as he drove. Although he was busy driving, I knew he could feel my eyes on him. How could he not with the bad vibes I kept sending his way?

As soon as I heard his voice, I realized who he was. The deep tones of his voice contrasted with his somewhat soft features.

His hair appeared to be almost the same shade as mine, just slightly paler. Now that the darkness in his eyes had receded, his irises were chocolate brown. Though he must have been in his late forties, I saw no evidence of wrinkles, no doubt a result of using black magic to retain his youthful appearance. He might be handsome for an old guy, but I still didn't trust his ass.

"I'm not a threat, Ruby," he suddenly declared.

I rolled my eyes. "Well, we both know that's bullshit, since you actually threatened to kill me," I contended. I didn't understand his intentions at all. This man had threatened to kill me when he visited me in Axel's dungeon, so why had he bothered to save me when that vampire had almost drained me dry? Nothing made sense in this supernatural world.

The only reason I had gotten into this damn car in the first place was because Axel asked me to. Presley and his men were out of commission, and it wouldn't have been wise for us to stay out in the open. Xavier was already uneasy with asking a black magic user for help, so he shared my discomfort with the situation. He rode in the backseat with me while Axel sat in front with the warlock.

"What?" Xavier questioned, clearly puzzled. "How do you two know each other?"

"When Axel kidnapped me, this guy showed up in the dungeon where I was being kept. He knew about our mate bond and that it could never be discovered. His dislike for me was clear then, so I'm not sure what game he's playing now."

Axel looked over at the warlock angrily.

"I have no intentions of hurting Ruby now—you can trust me on that," the warlock quickly told him.

"How did you know about the mate bond?" Axel probed.

The warlock smiled. "I have my ways," he answered with a smirk.

I huffed in disgust. "Ways of being a creep, you mean," I muttered. "What's your angle? First, you wanted me dead. Now you're helping me... helping us. Why?"

He inhaled deeply and exhaled heavily. "Personal reasons drove me to say those things to you in that dungeon. At first, I thought a werewolf being mated to a human would only bring about heartache and pain. Now, however, I see that it's necessary."

"How so?" Xavier prodded him.

"Humans and werewolves will need to come together in order to defeat the vampires. What better way to prove werewolves and humans can work together successfully than a mate bond between the two species?" He shrugged his shoulders. "Besides, other supernaturals are staying out of this fight. Fighting the vampires separately won't do anyone any good. The vampires are turning more and more humans and supernaturals. If all supernaturals and humans stand together, we'll outnumber the vamps. It's a simple solution."

"Uniting all the species won't be an easy task," Xavier pointed out.

The warlock nodded in agreement.

The bastard hadn't even told us his name yet. I wouldn't be asking him though. I wouldn't want him to operate under the impression I was actually interested. Besides, Axel had been the one to call him, so he must know what this monster called himself.

I tilted my head to the side. On the other hand, maybe I should consider toning down my attitude. If he was a black magic user capable of helping me with the wall in my mind, he probably also had the power to make things easier on me in terms of paying the price for the dark magic. It was probably smarter to avoid giving him a reason to make it any harder on me than it needed to be. "It's not a bad idea, though," I interjected helpfully.

The warlock turned his head to the side, no doubt surprised I was agreeing.

Xavier looked over at me quizzically.

I shrugged. "What? You know it's not a bad idea, even though it came from him."

Well, I tried to be friendly, and that's what counts, right?

The warlock chuckled. "I like your spunk, Ruby. I always have. You have a backbone."

"Can you read minds?" I asked him.

"No, why?"

Fuck you, you motherfucking, red-headed, black magic using cocksucker!

I smiled innocently. "No reason."

"How did you know about our mate bond?" Xavier asked, refusing to let him get away with his previous vague non-answer.

Even though I sat in the back, the way his cheeks puffed out told me he was smirking yet again.

"Well," he drawled. "I used black magic, of course. Look, I know everyone has questions, and I can answer a few of them. I can't do that right now, though. We need to get to my place as soon as possible. I need to focus on driving, if you all don't mind."

"I mind," I replied as he ran a red light. I would have been shocked if he had stopped, but I was even more surprised the stop lights were working.

"I know you do," he quickly countered as if he had been expecting me to say that. "But there is a full moon tonight, so you two gentlemen won't be much help if we're attacked. Fending off a vampire attack right now, especially if it came from more than one vamp... well, let's just say that wouldn't be ideal. Not even my magic is that strong." He glanced over his shoulder quickly before looking back at the road. "Unless you decided to help out, Ruby."

"Her powers don't work like that, Malcolm. You know that," Axel grumbled.

So, his name is Malcolm. Huh, he doesn't look like a Malcolm to me.

"Well, maybe she would feel inclined to help if a vampire attacked her, wouldn't you, Ruby?" he asked.

I didn't say anything because I was lost in thought. Something just seemed so familiar about Malcolm. It wasn't just the times we'd met in the past. It was in the way he spoke, his hand gestures, and the way he smirked as if he always knew something you didn't.

"You seem familiar," I murmured to Malcolm.

He nodded. "Yes, we just talked about that."

"That wasn't what I meant." I narrowed my eyes at him. "There's something about you that's familiar. It's like deja vu, but with just your face." I leaned forward somewhat. "I met you before, didn't I?"

"Before?" he repeated.

I slapped my hand on my thigh. I felt like something was just within my reach, but I couldn't grab it. It was the same feeling I always got when I tried to think past the last memory I had. The feeling I got whenever Natalie tried to access my past. "I met you before I met Xavier, didn't I?"

He didn't reply.

Axel looked over at him. "Did you?"

"Maybe," Malcolm answered vaguely.

Axel turned to face him now.

I wrung my hands with worry. If I had met Malcolm before our meeting in the dungeon, he must have known who I was before. "Tell me," I ordered through clenched teeth. "You met me before. Tell me who I was then. Who are you? Do you know what's happening to me?" My eyes widened. "Was it you that blocked my memories?"

"It wasn't me. I don't know what's happening to you, Ruby, but I'm not surprised something is," he declared.

I frowned.

Xavier voiced my thoughts before I could. "What's that supposed to mean?"

Malcolm sighed and pinched the bridge of his nose. He then combed his hand through his hair.

I watched him with growing anxiety. "Can you please tell me who you are? I *know* you."

"Trust me, you'll want to talk about this once we get to my place," he answered after a moment.

My heart skipped a beat. I clenched my fists as my vision inexplicably changed. Suddenly, I could see Xavier and Axel's energy, a bright wavy white color. Yet Malcolm's energy was black mixed with white. I blinked, and it was gone. I could still feel it though. Whenever my emotions became more intense, it appeared to trigger one of my abilities. It seemed safe to conclude my powers were closely tied to my emotional state.

Right now, I was feeling pretty anxious. The longer Malcolm took to answer, the more nervous I became. My hand began to twitch, and the lights on the dashboard started to flicker.

Xavier reached over to hold my hand, but I pulled away.

Malcolm looked down at the blinking lights on the dashboard.

Axel looked around at me. "Are you doing this?" he asked me.

My attention was still focused on Malcolm. "Tell me," I demanded again, my voice low. "I need to know."

Malcolm sighed heavily. "Fine. I should seem familiar to

you, Ruby, but I had nothing to do with your memories being locked away. I didn't even know your memories were taken until I saw you much later after our first meeting, and you had no idea who I was. When we met originally, it was brief."

"None of that answers my questions!"

The car made a horrible sound.

Malcolm gripped the steering wheel tightly as the car swayed. "If I'm to tell you anything, you need to calm down!"

This man had some fucking nerve. First, he wanted to kill me. Then he saved my life—more than once, in fact. Next he admitted he possessed information about my past that Natalie and I'd been frying our brains in mind links for weeks trying to find.

Now he wants to hold out until we get to his house and has the balls to demand that I calm the fuck down until we get there? What the hell?

"Don't tell me to calm down! You have no idea what I'm going through right now! I want to know what you know—everything you know!"

The car bucked forward and stopped.

Malcolm slammed on the brakes. He turned around to face me. "You know me because I'm your father!"

Xavier

I wasn't the 'I told you so' type, but I so wanted to rub those words into Axel's face right about now. Malcolm hadn't told us the price for helping Ruby, but he had revealed something that might be worse than any payment he might have asked for.

Malcolm drove off again after dropping the 'I'm your father' bomb as if he hadn't just rocked Ruby's world. No one spoke as he drove.

Axel threw a look my way before looking at Ruby.

Her wide eyes hadn't left Malcolm since he'd revealed that he was her father.

Malcolm was a warlock who used black magic, but Natalie hadn't sensed magic like that within Ruby. What had he meant when he said he wasn't surprised she had powers? What had he done? Was his black magic the reason why Ruby was now developing powers?

"Stop," Ruby said softly. "Please stop," she said again, this time a little louder.

Seemingly ignoring her, Malcolm kept driving. His red hair, much like hers, swayed as he shook his head. "We can't keep stopping, Ruby. We can't be out here much longer. It's too dangerous," he warned.

This man couldn't be serious. How could he be so oblivious right now? Then again, I had sensed it from the moment I'd met him—an emptiness about him. After all, he had threatened to kill her—his very own daughter.

"Stop the fucking car!" she screamed at the top of her lungs.

Again, the lights on the dashboard began to flicker.

I reached out and gently placed a hand on her thigh as she hunched forward and held her head with a moan. "Ruby, listen to me…" I whispered to her.

She only smacked my hand away. When she looked up at me, a tear fell from her eye. "Stay away from me," she directed through clenched teeth. Her eyes then drifted to Malcolm. Her face twisted with pain as she stared at him. "Stop! Stop! Let me out! Stop! STOP!"

Suddenly, we all rushed to cover our faces as the glass in Malcolm's window shattered to pieces. The car swayed and then skidded to a halt.

Ruby jumped out of the car quicker than I was able to grab her. "Ruby!" I yelled after her.

Axel jumped out of the car to follow her.

I opened my door and Malcolm did the same.

As Ruby ran towards the forest, a cloud of smoke pulled her back.

I grabbed Malcolm's arm and pushed him back against the car. "Let her go!"

After a brief moment of hesitation, he retracted his magic.

Ruby spun around to face us.

"We don't have time to go chasing after her in the woods!" Malcolm exclaimed.

"You piece of shit!" Ruby shouted.

When I looked back at her—I deliberately did a double-take. I blinked my eyes rapidly as I wondered if something was affecting my vision.

Her eyes were flashing from black to green. It was the same black as her father's or mine, the black of supernatural power. It represented yet another new manifestation of her growing abilities.

When Axel stepped forward, she pinned him with a glare that could freeze water. "Stay away from me," she whispered. Although she spoke at a quiet volume, the threat and anger in her voice were unmistakable. She looked over at Malcolm. "You're my father. If you've changed your mind about wanting to kill me, why not reveal yourself and tell me what I am? Tell me who I am! You've been lurking around while my life was being ruined!" Her eyes changed to black and remained that way. As her voice rose in volume, her scent grew stronger. That sweet aroma would draw vampires to us very soon. Her head twitched, and she winced as she held her head. "It hurts," she groaned.

Axel took another step towards her.

Malcolm stopped him.

"What's happening to her?" Axel demanded.

Malcolm moved towards her slowly. "I shouldn't have told her I'm her father. She was getting worked up already but…" He sighed, as he looked her up and down. "It was time to tell her the truth."

Ruby snorted as the wind began to pick up around us. "It was time to tell me the truth, huh? You've had many chances to tell me the truth—countless maybe! You might have saved me from this entire fucked up situation if only I had known the truth. You could have answered so many questions I needed answered. I didn't need to have Natalie hammering inside my head! No, you weren't interested in telling me anything! You preferred to resort to killing me—your own daughter! What did I ever do to you, huh?" She pressed her finger into her temple. "Who blocked my memories? What's my real name?"

"Your real name *is* Ruby. I know you're angry, and you have every right to be. But listen to me... we can't stay here much longer. Just come with me, come with us, and I'll—"

"Fuck you!" She screamed as her gorgeous red hair swirled around her, though no wind blew to whip it up.

I looked closer and realized her hair was actually floating, almost as if she was submerged in water.

"You're lying, and I'm not getting into that car! You're not my father. You can't be."

Malcolm took another step closer to her. "I am your father, Ruby. It's the truth. I can prove it, and I can help you get your memories back. I'll tell you everything you want to know. I just need you to calm down!" He held his hands up. "I won't hurt you. Do you honestly think Axel and Xavier would let me? I can feel your magic, Ruby. It's unstable, and you're losing control. Just breathe for me."

Axel leaned his head back and inhaled deeply before looking my way. "They're coming. I can smell them."

I turned to Ruby and held my hands up.

When she turned to me, her features softened somewhat and her pitch black eyes glossed over with unshed tears. "Xavier," she pleaded in a wounded voice.

I nodded my head to her. "I know, babe, I know you're angry. You can smell them, can't you? Vampires are coming, and we don't know how many. We can't stay here. The stronger you get, the stronger your scent becomes."

She opened her mouth to say something, but hunched forward instead as she held her head. She began groaning in pain, and her body began to shake. When she stood up, her face was covered in sweat, and her eyes were squeezed shut. "Make them stop. It's too much!"

"What's too much?" I asked.

Her eyes opened a little and squinted, as if it was too painful for her to open them all the way. "Pictures, flashing pictures—I can see it all. I can see me." She held her head with both hands. "Xavier, make them stop!"

"Help her," I growled to Malcolm. This was his fault. After all, he could have told her something else, anything else, just to get her off his back until we had reached his house.

Malcolm, however, said nothing, as he looked her up and down. "I didn't know her powers were growing so rapidly," he whispered to himself. He kept staring at her as if she was an animal at a zoo. "How has she gotten this strong this quickly?"

I grew irritated. We didn't have time for this. She was in pain, and the more power she used, the harder it would be for her to calm down.

Axel yelled impatiently, "How about you keep your curiosity to yourself and fucking help her? We need to go!"

We stepped back swiftly as the ground around Ruby cracked.

"Shut up!" she shrieked, as the ground cracked further. "Stop talking about me as if I'm not standing right here." She raised her hand.

Malcolm was sent flying back against the car, enough to push the car away. He fell to the ground.

Ruby stepped forward as the ground beneath her feet continued cracking. "You abandoned me," she accused through clenched teeth, "Do you know how hard my life has been? I've had no one since the day I was born. I have no idea where I come from, nothing!"

Malcolm then got to his feet.

I watched as red lines began to spread up her arms, and Axel and I stepped back.

Not Malcolm—he stepped forward.

Crowding her wasn't helping. If we could've shifted, Axel and I might have been capable of subduing her. Unfortunately, that wasn't an option tonight. If she lashed out now, we wouldn't heal as quickly under this full moon. Trying to physically control her now—when she could burn us from the inside out—would be foolish.

"I didn't know about you, Ruby... not until it was too late. I didn't know I had a daughter. I didn't know you existed."

Ruby froze, and the air temperature around us started to rise precipitously. Suddenly, Ruby raised her hand toward Malcolm again.

This time, Malcolm's head quickly whipped to the side as if he'd just received a slap from an invisible hand.

I internally noted the odor of vampire stench growing ever stronger, and I prayed we could somehow get Ruby under control before we had a group of bloodthirsty vampires surrounding us.

I felt useless watching Ruby like this. I wished I could do something to help her, to calm her down. Ultimately, I understood this was something between a father and daughter. He was far more capable of helping her than me.

Malcolm faced Ruby, as his hand fell limply away from his cheek to reveal a long gash now visible across his face. After dripping blood that looked black instead of red, it began to heal quickly.

I'd always avoided black magic users in the past because I didn't trust them, so I guess it wasn't so surprising that I had no idea their blood was black.

When he'd been shot earlier, Malcolm had healed before he had even started to bleed.

I hadn't given much thought to it then, but it was just more evidence of what he was.

His eyes turned black, and his features hardened. The darkness I'd suspected lurking beneath his skin and hidden behind his soft-spoken voice revealed itself as he hissed at Ruby. "Fuck it."

Axel rushed forward to attack him.

I charged forward as well. I wasn't sure what he was about to do, but I felt like it wouldn't be anything good. His entire body turned to smoke as he passed through Axel and me. A cold chill surged through my body as he went through me. I glanced down at my hands to find that black smoke was making its way up my body from my feet.

I tried to turn but doing so took more effort than it should. The same was happening to Axel. When I finally managed to look Ruby's way, Malcolm held his arms wide, and she was covered in smoke.

"Ruby!" I shouted as the smoke began to vanish along with her. I couldn't believe what I was seeing. "Ruby!" My nostrils began to burn with the vampire's scent, but as I looked down at my body, the smoke now to my chest, I too was vanishing. A metallic taste sprang to my mouth as the smoke reached Axel's and my throat. Then I heard the loud hisses of vampires.

A male vampire ran out of the woods, his eyes blood red with his mouth open wide as he growled. The smoke engulfed my head, and the vampire passed right through me, as did another one that charged at Axel.

My vision started to blur, but I counted four other vampires before my vision went completely black. My sense of touch and sight was gone entirely, and I was surrounded by an impenetrable darkness. I strained my ears to listen for a sound, but I heard nothing. I also couldn't move my body with the exception of my hands. All I could do was clench my fists as my body started to move as if I was floating.

My heart hammered in my chest, but panicking wouldn't help me out of this place—wherever this was. The moment we made it out of this nothingness, I would be punching Axel in the balls for creating this mess by calling Black Magic Malcolm in the first place. At this point, I felt like we'd have been better off with the humans.

I landed suddenly with a loud oomph, and I heard Axel touch down with a satisfying thump somewhere nearby. I rolled to my side and got up quickly while shaking my head, the darkness in front of my eyes fading slowly. The first thing I noticed was the soft crackle of a fireplace.

When my eyes cleared, I turned to my left to find a healthy fire roaring in a massive fireplace. I quickly surveyed the rest of my surroundings—luxe black leather sofas, thick grey carpet, and three swords hanging above the fireplace.

Axel was scanning our new environment as well.

"Where are we?" I asked.

Axel shrugged. "I don't know, but we need to get out of here and find Ruby. I should never have trusted that fucker. Did we just teleport?"

The sound of boots approaching caught our attention, and we both moved into a fighting stance.

"Yes, you both just teleported," Malcolm explained as he rounded a corner, a glass of water in hand. He took a sip, waved his hand, and two other glasses of water appeared on the coffee table between Axel and me. "You both should drink something. You won't notice it until I say this, but you're both very thirsty."

I suddenly felt parched, as if I hadn't tasted water in a century. If I had planned to reject his offer of water, there was no way I would now.

Axel and I dove towards the glasses. We finished our drinks in one long gulp, and the glasses magically refilled.

We finished them again.

"This water better not be poisoned," Axel grumbled as he downed his third glass of water before turning to Malcolm.

"Where is Ruby?" I asked as I stepped forward, the glass in my hand cracking as I squeezed it.

Malcolm raised his right hand. The glass in his hand fell and vanished before it could hit the ground. Our glasses vanished as well. "Ruby is fine, I assure you. No, Axel, the water wasn't poisoned. We couldn't stay out there much longer, so I had no choice but to ask for help."

I narrowed my eyes at him. "Ask for help? From whom?"

That smirk I so hated returned to his lips. "You'll find out soon enough." He held his arms out as his smile widened. "Welcome to my home. Come on, I'll take you to Ruby. She's still unconscious."

9

RUBY

I opened my eyes, and all I could see was white. I got up off the floor unsteadily, my body feeling as if all my energy had been drained away.

"What the hell?" I wondered aloud as I turned in a circle. I was in a white padded cell with no door. "Hello!" I shouted, but it sounded like my voice was only bouncing around the room.

"Hello!" I yelled again, as I started to panic.

The last thing I remembered was Malcolm coming at me and engulfing me in his black smoke. I stopped pacing as I remembered the vision I'd been having, the one with the wolves engulfed by black smoke and the cobra.

Maybe the black smoke in my vision was Malcolm. If so, what did the wolf and the cobra mean?

I pressed my fingers to my temples, massaging them as I felt a headache coming on. "Hello!" I shouted a little louder as I placed my hands on my knees. "Malcolm? I know you can hear me."

The sound of a door opening met my ears, and I spun

around to find Malcolm staring at me with his hands in his pockets. "Have you calmed down?"

This man has some serious issues.

"You locked me in a padded cell. Let's see how much longer I'm going to remain calm if you keep me in here."

"Are you calm?" he asked once again.

I sighed deeply. "Yes. Where are we?" I questioned. "Where are Xavier and Axel?"

Malcolm stepped to the side and held his hand out as if gesturing towards an open door. "You're free to leave. You'll be able to see them."

I narrowed my eyes at him, but trying to read him was a waste of time. I stepped forward and walked past him indignantly. He was so high on my shit list right now I doubted he could ever work his way off of it, and I wasn't about to let him forget it.

In the blink of an eye, my surroundings changed completely. I suddenly found myself lying down on a comfortable bed in a spacious and brightly lit bedroom.

Axel and Xavier were both standing over me while Malcolm sat in a nearby chair with his legs crossed.

I sat up abruptly.

So I was sleeping the whole time?

I filed that away in my mind as I swung my legs off the bed. "You're a real piece of work, you know that?" I informed Malcolm.

He nodded. "So I've been told several times," he admitted with a chuckle. "You might have a headache for a while."

"Here," Xavier directed as he handed me a glass of water. "You don't feel thirsty, do you?"

The moment he said that to me, I instantly felt parched. I

grabbed the glass of water from him and began chugging it down. I didn't think I'd ever been this thirsty in my whole life. I was about to ask for some more water when the glass filled up on its own. I narrowed my eyes at it and then looked at Malcolm. I wanted to reject the new glass of water, but I couldn't. "Why am I so thirsty?"

"The magic I used to teleport us here had its price. Let's just leave it at that," Malcolm responded.

I sent a confused look Xavier's way.

"The same happened to us," he informed me as he pointed at Axel and then himself. "How are you feeling?"

"My powers are under control." I smiled at him with a hint of embarrassment. "Sorry about it taking—wait, how long have I been out?"

"About an hour is all," Malcolm answered.

I handed the glass back to Xavier, but my face twisted at the pulsating pain in my head. "Why is my head hurting so much?" I questioned.

Malcolm got up and left the room.

As I watched him leave, I had a brief vision of the shadowy snake's beady eyes. I felt a sudden chill and it was gone as Malcolm closed the door.

I hate snakes.

I still can't believe he's my father. How could he be? Why would he lie about something like that? Other than his red hair, there wasn't anything else that showed any kind of family resemblance. I looked around the room at the black and dark red theme while narrowing my eyes. I eyed a painting beside the door that looked like blood running down a window and puckered my lips thoughtfully.

Okay, we had the same taste in terms of décor color, but that didn't mean anything.

Did it?

I wasn't sure how to feel. He was my father, but I felt nothing towards him. Well, nothing *good* towards him. I did feel something though... anger and confusion. He had explained why he changed his mind about wanting to kill me, but why had he wanted me dead to begin with? How could he, especially knowing that I was his flesh and blood?

Had I done something so horrible even my own father hated me, and I just couldn't remember doing it?

"Ruby?" Xavier said, his dark eyes watching me with concern.

I looked up at him.

"Did you guys get headaches too?" I inquired.

Xavier shook his head.

"No," Axel responded. "I'm not surprised you did, though. You certainly put on a show earlier, Red."

I gave him a tight-lipped smile. "Yeah, I guess so." When my powers were triggered earlier, it seemed the angrier I got, the more I felt the energy. The more I felt the magic, the more I wanted it. I felt powerful, more powerful than I ever had in my life. It actually felt amazing.

Something about it was also scary, though. What if my power controlled me, instead of me controlling it? What if I gave into that euphoric feeling and became addicted? After how good I had felt when I used it last time, a part of me couldn't wait until I used my magic again. Becoming addicted seemed possible. "I've never felt anything like that," I whispered. "I felt in control. I felt unbeatable—right up until

Malcolm engulfed me in smoke and I couldn't see anything anymore, that is."

"Your eyes changed to black," Axel informed me. "They were black like Malcolm's and ours. I've never seen you do that before."

I frowned, as I looked his way.

"Same with the red veins running up your arms," Xavier added.

"I don't know about my eyes, but when my powers triggered during Axel and Presley's argument back at the house, I noticed the veins on my wrists were bright red," I told them.

"Here," Malcolm offered as he entered the room.

I stared at the brown liquid in the glass he was handing to me.

"It'll help with the headache," he said.

I arched a brow at him and hesitated.

He sighed and took a sip. "See, it's not poison. I don't want to hurt you, Ruby."

I took the glass from him. "So you keep saying." I pinched my nose before swiftly gulping down the unpleasant smelling concoction.

Malcolm returned to his seat across the room and explained calmly, "You were losing it and calling vampires to us in the process. Arguing with you was wasting time, so I acted. Now here we are. On the plus side, we were able to avoid two hours of driving. We can fight all you want here, but not out there, where we could be attacked at any moment."

I watched as a snake appeared from behind his chair to slither down his arm. I shot a meaningful look at Xavier and

Axel before cocking my head in the direction of the snake. I was hoping they'd remember the vision I'd told them about, although the cobra in my vision had been significantly bigger. "Interesting pet choice," I mumbled before looking Malcolm's way. "Why do you have a pet cobra?"

"He's not a pet," he replied.

Axel stepped over to the bed and sat down beside me. "Why didn't Natalie sense magic like yours within Ruby?" he asked Malcolm. "If you're her father, it would explain her powers. I've never seen a warlock or witch with her abilities, though."

"That's because she doesn't have witch magic." Malcolm got up and moved away to turn his back to us. "You see... I wasn't born a warlock." He turned around to face us once more. "I was born human, like Ruby."

"I'm sorry, what?" Axel sputtered as he crossed his arms over his chest. "How did a human manage to acquire magic, especially strong black magic like yours?"

"Easy," Malcolm replied with a shrug of his shoulders. "I tied my soul to a shadow demon."

My brows dipped as I frowned. "The cobra?" I guessed.

Malcolm nodded. "Yes, it's a shadow demon, not a pet cobra."

"Why would you do that?" I asked, bemused.

Malcolm smiled sadly.

I suspected it was the most genuine expression he'd shown since we'd met, or should I say... met again.

He returned to his chair and reclined in it, his finger pressed against his temple and a distant look in his eyes. "Your mother and I were in love."

My face dropped as I stared blankly at the mention of my

mother. While I felt no connection to Malcolm, even hearing a mere reference to my mother had my heart beating a mile a minute. I didn't know who she was, but knowing I was about to find out sent my anxiety sky high.

"One day, she vanished." Malcolm's unfocused eyes were glued to the floor as if he was seeing something else entirely. "She left without a warning or note. She simply disappeared. It was years later when I got a lead on her location. By the time I got there, it was already too late. I found out she had been pregnant when she left me, and..." he paused as he stared at me. "...she died while giving birth to a baby girl."

I was shocked at the pain within his eyes. I placed my hand over my heart as it skipped a beat. Growing up, I had thought of so many possible reasons for how I had ended up an orphan. At one point, I even convinced myself that my parents must have been murdered. Eventually, I came to accept the idea that most likely, my parents just didn't want me.

Yet, in all those years of imagining plausible scenarios, I never once thought of the possibility I had killed my own mother. I swallowed har. While I could see in my peripheral vision that Xavier and Axel had turned to gauge my reaction, I couldn't look at either of them right now. I would burst into tears.

I had killed my own mother.

I kept my eyes on Malcolm and our gazes locked. "Is that why you wanted to kill me? Because I killed the woman you loved?" I couldn't find it in me to say 'my mother.' I was a child, a baby, but because of me, my own mother lost her life.

"No," he told me as he shook his head. "That's not why I wanted to kill you." He placed his elbows on his knees as he leaned forward. "I wanted to kill you to prevent another human from falling in love with a wolf."

I was dumbfounded. "What?"

"Are you saying Ruby's mother was a werewolf?" Xavier asked, shock and disbelief evident in his voice.

It finally clicked.

I looked from Malcolm to Xavier and then back at Malcolm. "Is this true?"

"Yes," Malcolm affirmed.

I got up and walked away. I ran my hands down my head and hair, overwhelmed and confused by Malcolm's revelation.

Natalie had been sure I didn't have werewolf blood. According to her, my magic or blood was unlike any other supernatural creature she knew of. She probably had never come into contact with a hybrid werewolf-human child before, so that must be why she'd been wrong in her assessment.

"Yet, your mother was not an ordinary werewolf. She was an Enchanted," Malcolm stated.

I spun around to look him in the eye. I knew Enchanteds were descendants of the goddesses so did that mean…?

No… was I part human, part werewolf, and part demigod?

I held up my hands. "Hold on, just hold on, I…" I exhaled heavily. "…just slow down for a minute, okay? You said my mother was an Enchanted? What does that make me?"

Malcolm stood to his feet. "Yes, your mother was an Enchanted. She was a powerful one at that…an Elder, as I came to understand later. As for what that makes you, I can't—"

"Wait," Axel interjected as he pointed at Malcolm. "An Elder? You were in a relationship with an Enchanted Elder?"

Malcolm nodded, and from the look on his face, he knew what Axel was getting at.

This time, however, it didn't take me long to realize what was being said. I froze where I stood, praying Malcolm wouldn't say the name of the Elder I was thinking of.

"You're talking about Elder Lovette," Xavier concluded.

While it wasn't a question, Malcolm nodded.

I released the breath I'd been holding.

Malcolm looked my way.

I shook my head, telling him not to say it.

"Your mother was Elder Lovette."

I exhaled through my mouth slowly. In and out, I breathed, but my hands wouldn't stop shaking, and the tears wouldn't stop flowing. I clenched my fists and then my jaw as I held my head up. "Lovette is my mother, huh?" I pinched the bridge of my nose while nodding. "Okay," I swallowed and looked back at Malcolm. "How? I want to know everything from the start."

Malcolm rubbed at his eye uncomfortably.

I didn't care how this made him feel. "I need to know, and you said you'd tell me everything. I want to know about her—"

"I didn't know her as Lovette," he replied, suddenly cutting me off. "When I met her, she went by a different name. When she vanished, I searched everywhere for her, but it was pointless because the woman I knew didn't exist." He chuckled, but there was no humor in it. "Do you know how I found her? I was walking by what appeared to be a shady fortune teller's shop one day during the course of my search for your mother. The fortune teller opened the door the moment I walked by. She stopped me and announced she could help me find what I was searching for. Of course, I thought she was just messing with me. After all, how could she know I was looking for something? How would she have known to exit her shop the exact moment I was walking by?" He rubbed his hands together before placing them palms down on the handles of his black wingback chair. "It turned out that the shady fortune teller was actually a real witch. She helped me to find what happened to Lovette. Unfortunately, by then it was too late. You had already been born, and she was dead. I was in a three year long relationship with the Grand Elder of a species I didn't even know existed. She died, and I realized I never really knew her at all."

For the first time since meeting this man, this warlock... my father, I felt sorry for him. I looked at Xavier and didn't even want to imagine the pain I'd feel if I lost him.

Things had changed so much in our relationship that now... I even felt the same about Axel. He'd more than proven himself to me. Although I was closer to Xavier than I was with him, losing Axel would be just as painful.

Malcolm was feeling the pain of knowing Lovette and losing her, even if he had only known the version of her that she'd been able to show him at the time. I didn't know her at all, but knowing she had died because of me and that I wouldn't meet her the way I'd met Malcolm was like suddenly having a wound that might not ever fully heal. The pain would always be there, dull and aching.

"The witch couldn't locate you, Ruby," Malcolm went on. "So I took matters into my own hands. The witch told me progeny resulting from a human and Enchanted relationship was unheard of, especially one from an Elder. She believed it must have been why Lovette died and that you couldn't have survived either, but I couldn't give up there. I needed to know if you were alive or not. Desperate and out of options, I finally asked a demon for help. Tying myself to the demon was the price to find you, and I paid it. You were all I had left of Lovette."

"Then why did you want to kill me?" I asked, still confused. I felt I'd asked this question too many times already. "Why? You don't hate me because Lovette died giving birth to me, so what? What did I do?"

"I watched over you for years. Then everything changed for me when you met Xavier." Malcolm looked at Xavier and shook his head. "I couldn't let what happened to Lovette and me happen to you too. Humans and werewolves don't mix. I thought if your bond were ever discovered, some other werewolves might think being with a human would work out. They'd look for their mates not only just among wolves, but also among humans too." He stared at Axel and then me. "What would happen when more and more humans learned about werewolves? It'd be only a matter of time before they discovered witches, warlocks, demons, and all other manner of supernaturals out there." He held his hands up and dropped them back down on the arms of his chair. "I knew it would mean chaos and death, and I wasn't wrong. It ended up happening anyways, it just had nothing to do with your mate bond, Ruby. I…" He sighed deeply. "As selfish as it might sound, I thought you'd be better dead than to be the cause of a war between humans and supernaturals."

"I don't know," Axel replied as he shrugged. "Maybe this is just me, but I feel like there were plenty of other options you could have thought of other than killing her." His condescending tone came out crystal clear as he dug his hands into his pockets.

Xavier's head bobbed in agreement.

I didn't know what to say. I stood there quietly, Malcolm's words still repeating in my mind about Lovette, the demon, and his reason for wanting to kill me. He had tried to protect me, but his means of doing so were twisted. I took a deep breath and walked back to the bed to sit down. I sat there as the silence within the room stretched on.

"Natalie checked Ruby," Axel suddenly announced. "And she has no traces of werewolf or Enchanted magic. Lovette couldn't have been her mother."

I looked away from the spot on the floor that had held my attention as my mind wandered.

"Trust me, she is," Malcolm insisted. "There are puzzle pieces still missing, but Ruby is most definitely my daughter. This means her mother can't be anyone else other than Lovette. Yet, the powers Ruby has didn't come from Lovette or me. That means I need to know what's hidden in her mind as much as you three do."

Natalie and Reika had insisted they had seen Lovette within my memories, and she had been crying. *Maybe I had indeed met Lovette, but how? How could I have a memory of a woman who died when I was born?*

"I can do the spell now, if you're ready," Malcolm offered.

While they spoke, I kept staring at the locked door.

"What's the price?" Xavier questioned cautiously.

"Just blood—her blood. I'll be doing blood magic, so that'll be all," Malcolm explained.

"I'm ready," I said softly. I was already overloaded with

information, but I couldn't wait any longer to know what happened in my past. I had to know.

Malcolm got up. "I just need to gather a few things. I think it would be best if we do this in the living room." He left us alone.

No one spoke.

Neither Axel nor Xavier said anything to me.

I felt grateful for the silence. The last thing I wanted to be asked right now was if I was okay. I didn't want their sympathy or their pity.

We walked to the massive living room in silence.

The cobra locked in an enormous glass cage caught my attention immediately. I studiously avoided looking into its eyes, particularly now that I knew it was a demon.

Within the middle of the room was a large circle drawn with white chalk. There were symbols and writing I didn't recognize within it. At its center sat a small black bowl.

"Please step inside the circle," Malcolm instructed me politely.

I looked at Xavier and then Axel, like a child being told to do something but needing approval from their parents.

Axel moved a strand of my hair behind my ears, and Xavier nodded reassuringly.

I inhaled deeply and held my breath as I stepped into the circle.

"Stand at the center, Ruby," Malcolm directed.

I released the breath I was holding and did as he told me.

He stepped into the circle as well.

I did a 360 turn as the red candles outside the circle lit on their own. I turned back around to face Malcolm.

Without warning, he grabbed my hand and sliced my palm with a knife.

I screamed and tried pulling away, but his hold on my hand tightened.

Axel and Xavier stepped forward as Malcolm held my clenched fist over the black bowl.

I grimaced as I watched my blood drain into the container.

After a moment, he forced me to open my palm, and he waved his hand over mine.

I marveled at how the wound had completely vanished as if it had never been there at all. I still pinned Malcolm with a glare as he twirled my blood around in the bowl. "You could have warned me," I snapped at him.

He didn't seem to care as he merely kept gazing into the bowl. "My way worked better," he replied calmly.

I took the time to observe him more closely. When he looked at me, I realized his pupils weren't round but instead had a slight elliptical shape—similar to a cat or snake, but more subtle.

He released his grip on the bowl.

My hands shot out to catch it before it fell. However, it remained effortlessly suspended in the air, and I gave Malcolm a dead stare. I opted for saying and doing nothing while I watched as he pressed the knife into his palm and cut himself.

I frowned as his black blood poured in and the contents of the bowl began to bubble.

He rubbed his fingers against his palm, and the wound vanished just as mine had. He plucked the floating bowl out of thin air.

I tried to keep a straight face as he drank the bubbling liquid. I swallowed hard. My mouth turned downward in disgust as he closed his eyes as if he enjoyed the taste.

When his eyes reopened, they were as black as a starless night sky.

This time when he dropped the bowl, I only watched as it fell instead of trying to catch it.

Again, without warning, Malcolm grabbed my head roughly with both hands.

When I gazed into his eyes, I gasped as the world around us fell away, replaced by a hospital room.

His hands dropped from my head, and I surveyed my surroundings.

Frantic nurses were running around like headless chickens.

A woman's piercing scream rang through the room, as Malcolm stepped forward, his black eyes wide. "Lovette," he mumbled under his breath.

I looked at the crying woman on the table.

Her pure white hair looked matted in some areas and tangled in others, her face covered in sweat. Her cheeks were bright red from exertion as she bit down and groaned in pain.

"Mom," I whispered under my breath as I stepped towards her.

"Just one more push, one more big push!" the doctor between her legs yelled.

As Lovette screamed, the lights and equipment started to flicker.

"She's doing it again!" the nurse to my right shouted.

"Focus!" the doctor admonished. "If this baby doesn't

come out soon, they will both die. She's lost too much blood!"

My heart kept hammering in my chest, my palms sweaty and my knees growing weak. I never in a million years imagined I'd watch my own birth. Here I was though, staring at my beautiful mother and the pain she suffered to give birth to me.

I looked away when Lovette pushed and screamed. Looking back again, I saw the top of a baby's head crowning.

However, Lovette stopped pushing and fell back onto the bed, panting. "I can't," she moaned as she shook her head from side to side.

"I love you so much," Malcolm said.

When I looked back, he was trying to hold Lovette's hand, but his hand only passed through hers like smoke.

"The baby's heartbeat is dropping fast!" a nurse yelled.

The doctor cursed loudly. "We have no choice, Ms. Lovette, we have to do a C-section."

A loud alarm blared in the room, and the nurses went into a frenzy.

"We're losing them! Both of them!"

I felt panicked. The urge to jump in and help caused my fingers to tingle. I looked over at Malcolm, surprised to see a black tear rolling down his cheek.

He was breathing hard, his shoulders rising and falling rapidly.

I wasn't sure if time had jumped forward, but the room went quiet, as all the nurses and the doctor were just staring at Lovette and a bundle wrapped in her arms.

The baby was still.

When Lovette moved the blanket away and picked up the

baby's hand, it looked pale, deathly pale. Lovette sobbed weakly.

I swiftly walked around to the side where the baby was and felt shocked to my core at what I saw.

I was dead.

"How? I-I don't understand," I said as I looked to Malcolm for answers.

He looked back at me with the same confusion.

"I died?"

"You will live," Lovette said weakly.

Her sweet singsong voice sounded like music to my ears.

One of Lovette's tears fell onto my little forehead. "Save her, save her, and not me."

My eyes stung as I suddenly started to cry.

"Oh my god, the baby's alive!"

I stepped closer to see myself as a baby, face red as I cried.

Lovette smiled weakly, her eyes now barely open. "I'm sorry. Your life will—will be hard, my beautiful girl. But—you'll save—so many lives." Lovette's head fell back and she flatlined.

I felt sick as this all unfolded in front of me.

"Lovette!" Malcolm yelled, but his multiple attempts to grab her were futile. None of this was real. There was a time many years ago when it had been, but right now, it was all a memory.

Tears rolled down my cheeks as the doctors tried to save Lovette, but she was dead.

I started bawling as I held my head. "Enough! Enough! I've seen enough."

Malcolm wasn't listening to me. He was lost in the memory, his eyes wide with his cheeks black from his tears.

"Malcolm!" I screamed. "I can't watch her die! Stop this, stop!" I pressed a nail into my wrist and winced as blood sprang to the surface.

We both woke up abruptly, and I looked around the room frantically before rushing out of the circle.

"No!" Malcolm roared, and the cobra in the cage began to hiss loudly. "No! I need to go back!" He rushed at me.

I waved my hand, sending him flying back. "I hate you!" I ran from the room, ignoring Axel's and Xavier's call.

All I could think about was how it felt to watch the life leaving my mother's eyes.

AXEL

I found Ruby sniffling and wiping her tears away in a room filled with animal wall hangings. I flinched as I saw the taxidermied wolf heads and furs, but at least they belonged to normal wolves and not werewolves.

Malcolm is one sick fuck.

While I could sympathize with him and his pain of losing Lovette, that was as far as it went. He had wanted to kill Ruby because he didn't want her to experience what he had, but that wasn't his decision to make. Everyone's life was filled with mistakes, poor choices, small victories, and everything in between. It was all theirs and theirs alone to face.

We all get help on our life's journey, but killing someone to avoid something we *thought* might happen to them was ridiculous. I understood the chain reaction he had spoken of, but there were so many ways to prevent that.

The epic interspecies war he wanted to kill Ruby in order to avoid happened anyways and was much worse than he had imagined. The girl he had wanted to kill now actually had the power to destroy the ones who started this war.

"Ruby?" I said as I approached her.

Her sniffling stopped and she stiffened, as if she'd just now heard me come into the room.

"Talk to me, Red." I walked around the sofa to face her, and my heart dropped at the sight of her bloodshot eyes.

Her face was soaked with tears. Her expression twisted with pain as more tears rolled down her cheeks.

My heart went out to her, and I dropped onto the sofa beside her to pull her into my arms.

As she sobbed, she clutched at my shirt as if her life depended on it.

The wall protecting my heart against her suddenly crumbled. I closed my eyes and kissed the top of her head as she cried. She felt so small in my arms, but I knew her small frame belied the size of her kind heart and luminous spirit.

Malcolm had vanished into the wall in a cloud of smoke after Ruby ran off, leaving Xavier and me to wonder what the fuck was happening. Xavier had wanted to look for Ruby, but I told him I'd find her and he needed to find Malcolm.

Finding her wasn't hard. Her scent was now hard to miss. Before leaving this place, Malcolm needed to make a potion to block her scent, or we wouldn't get a mile at night without being attacked by vampires.

I didn't have any idea where our next destination would be after this. Whatever alliance was created with Presley and his people was now nullified. I wasn't sure where to go from here.

Ruby pulled away from me and sighed as she wiped at her eyes.

I moved her hair back from her face. In the beginning, I judged her to be a weak human, unworthy of being my mate.

Even though she cried in my arms now, I'd seen her strength and determination time and time again throughout this whole ordeal. "What did you see?" I asked her.

She closed her eyes for a moment. When she reopened them, they were glossy with fresh unshed tears, but she composed herself. "Lovette—I saw Lovette—she-she was giving birth."

She looked at me with such raw sadness my heart constricted as if I could feel her pain, and I reached out to caress her cheek.

"S-she was giving birth to me," Ruby went on. "She's really my mother."

I felt like there was more, so I said nothing.

Ruby swallowed and looked away, a distant look in her eyes as if she remembered something.

"I died," she stated.

I frowned. "What?"

She sighed. "I died. The delivery was a difficult one, and I —died." She turned to gaze my way again as her brows dipped with confusion. "She said, 'Save her, save her and not me,' and I—I came back to life."

I narrowed my eyes. "So, the doctors helped to bring you back or—"

"I just came back to life," she interjected.

My frown deepened.

A person coming back to life wasn't unheard of in the supernatural world. Still, it was extremely rare. Essentially it was giving life, something only gods and Necromancers did, and Necromancers paid a high cost for the privilege.

"That's strange, yes," I replied.

Ruby gave me a look that said 'no shit.' "She said something else. She said my life is going to be hard, but I'm going to save many lives. What do you think she meant by that?"

I shrugged. Maybe Lovette had known about the powers Ruby would develop. Perhaps, she had even known about the vampire invasion, but how? I knew Enchanteds had the ability to see the future, but I'd never heard of any who could see it so far in advance.

Enchanteds also didn't have the power to bring anyone or anything back to life. If Lovette wasn't able to save Ruby herself, then who had?

"I don't know," I replied. "But considering what's happening now with your vampire frying powers, I would say she wasn't wrong."

"She died right after she said that," Ruby murmured as she palmed her face. "I watched her die. She died because of me." She sniffled loudly.

I moved her hair over her shoulder. "No, she didn't," I told her and I acted without thinking as I kissed her shoulder.

She startled, her eyes wide as she stared at me.

I stared back at her, a little surprised at myself, but I didn't regret it. She was my mate and she always would be. So of course, I was attracted to her. Of course, I wanted to feel her skin on mine and her lips against mine, but she was Xavier's more than she was mine. Of course, that was also my fault.

I had mistreated her in the beginning. "We both don't have the full story, but it's clear she saved your life. You didn't kill her, Ruby. From what you've said, like a good mother, she gave up her life for yours."

I placed my hand on her cheek, and swallowed hard as my wolf awakened. Being close to her and not being able to touch her was sometimes painful. My wolf yearned for her, but because of the way I treated her before, I kept denying him the chance to ever get close to her. "I know you're hurting and not much I say will make you feel better. But tell me this: did your mother seem angry about saving you and not herself?"

Ruby stiffened and shook her head. "No."

"Did she not seem relieved when you came back to life?"

She nodded, her green eyes not looking away from my black ones. "Yes, she did."

"Then she didn't die in pain. She died happy, knowing she had saved her only child. You're the daughter of Lovette, the most beloved Enchanted Elder. Ruby, that's an honor you and only you hold."

She smiled.

Even if it was only a slight smile, I felt proud that I had been able to help put it there. Ruby had witnessed a horrible thing, one that would haunt her for a while, but maybe she'd hold onto the good in the situation. "You also know where you come from. That's one puzzle piece found."

"Thanks," she murmured.

I rubbed my hand against her cheek. "Anytime, Ruby."

"Are you okay? Why are your eyes black?" she asked as she reached a hand out to my face.

The moment her fingers touched my face, I kissed her. The restraint—I'd been holding back for so long—just broke. My wolf howled with joy the moment she didn't pull away or slap me but instead leaned into the kiss. Her lips tasted better than I'd ever imagined, and I snaked my hand around her to pull her closer to me. It wasn't a gentle kiss—I'd never been good at being kind—but she matched my urgency and vigor, my need to taste as much of her as I could. Her lips were so incredibly soft.

When I felt my fangs descending, I feared I'd hurt her. I broke our liplock to kiss her cheek, chin, and then neck. She moaned softly, and I captured her lips once more for her to moan into my mouth.

She pulled away, her breathing now labored as she stared at me.

Perfect, she's perfect.

I swallowed hard and removed my hand from around her waist. "Sorry, I…"

She stared behind me, however.

When I turned around, Xavier stood at the door watching us.

Fuck. Wait, why should I care? She's my mate as well. He must have known that eventually Ruby and I would grow close. The mate bond wouldn't allow us to stay apart for too long.

She got up with a look on her face that I couldn't quite understand.

She walked over to him, stood on her tippy toes, and kissed Xavier as well.

It wasn't as heated as our kiss, and while I felt a stab of jealousy, it wasn't as strong as I had expected it to be.

When she pulled away, Xavier cupped her cheeks, the love in his eyes evident as he pulled her in for a hug.

This scenario was never what I expected when I found my mate, but here we were. I was watching my mate kiss another man, and unbelievably, my wolf didn't want to shred him to pieces.

Ruby pulled away and turned to face me. She looked a

little happier. Her cheeks stained red with a bright blush. "Is this as weird for you guys as it is for me?"

I nodded. "It's weird."

Xavier looked at me. "It is, but something we knew would happen sooner or later."

I didn't detect any hate or anger in his voice. Maybe a pinch of jealousy, but I felt the same, so I couldn't fault him for that.

"Are you okay?" he asked Ruby.

She nodded.

"What did you see?"

I listened as she told Xavier the same thing she'd told me.

Her eyes became glossy as she explained how her mother died.

Xavier consoled her. "Do you think you can continue?" he asked her. "I doubt that was the only memory locked away."

Ruby shrugged. "I don't know. I-if that was the first memory, I-I don't feel eager to see the others. Maybe my past was locked away for a reason... to protect me."

"True." I nodded. "But there might be things in your past that might be able to help you and us. Lovette is your mother, so Olcan won't be able to touch you now."

We all stared at Malcolm as he walked in.

Ruby smiled. "I'm really going to enjoy seeing the look on Olcan's face when he finds out." She crossed her arms over her chest.

Malcolm moved further into the room. His hair appeared tussled, and he still had black stains under his eyes.

During the ritual with Ruby, Xavier and I had watched as he'd cried in black blood.

"I understand you're angry, Ruby, but we have to continue," he said.

Ruby shook her head in disbelief.

I also felt shocked that after what he had just seen, after what Ruby had just been forced to witness, he'd want to continue so soon.

He sighed. "What we saw was only the tip of the iceberg. There is more to see. You died... something happened, or Lovette did something to bring you back. I need to know what. You were born human, but maybe coming back to life did something to you, and that's why you have the powers you do."

"How?" Ruby asked.

Malcolm shrugged. "I don't know. That's why we need to continue with the ritual."

Xavier crossed his arms, much like Ruby.

Ruby looked over at me.

I understood the uncertainty in her eyes. "Xavier and I will be there. Whatever you see, we'll be there."

She gazed at Xavier next.

He cupped her cheek. "We do need to know what else is hidden."

I didn't miss the curious look on Malcolm's face at the bond between Ruby and us.

He frowned for a moment before the expression disappeared.

Xavier looked his way and uncrossed his arms to bury his hands in his pockets. "We'll continue with the ritual, but not tonight. We can do it in the morning."

"Ruby is tired," I added.

Malcolm looked my way as the side of his mouth arched somewhat with a smirk.

I narrowed my eyes at him.

Malcolm bowed his head. "No problem. We'll continue at dawn. Pick whatever rooms you like." He turned to leave the room but not before pausing to look at each of us with a curious gaze. He then left the room.

Ruby turned away, her face in her hands. "That soulless man can't be my dad," she mumbled.

Xavier placed his hand on her back.

"He's your father Ruby, not your dad," I said.

She turned around and puckered her bottom lip.

I couldn't help smiling at how adorable she looked as I stated, "The title of Dad is earned."

"Yeah," she drawled. Her lips parted as if she intended to say something, but she changed her mind. "I do need to get some rest," she acknowledged with a slight yawn.

I stood up. "Well, goodnight," I said, knowing Xavier and her would be sleeping together. I'd just pick a room close to theirs in case I needed to get to Ruby quickly.

"Wait," she called.

I'd pulled my hair from its ponytail as I turned around. A long shower was definitely in order.

"Can you…" she paused and looked at Xavier.

He stared back at her in confusion.

Looking at me again, her cheeks were pink.

I frowned.

"Can you stay with me as well?" she asked in a small voice.

I raised a brow as Xavier and I eyed each other. I think

watching her kiss Xavier was enough for me for one night. "Um, I don't know, Ruby."

She stepped forward. "Please?"

How could I say no to that?

Unknown

I listened to the humans screams echoing from multiple rooms throughout the castle. Little did they know, no one would ever hear their cries. Their pitiful wailing was like sweet music to the ones who could actually hear them.

I stopped by an open door and looked inside, watching as a Bleeder stabbed a woman in her throat before latching onto her neck. It stuck its claws into the woman's gut and ripped her throat open with its fangs, its head leaning back as it licked its blood-coated lips.

The woman's teary eyes were on me, and she merely winced, almost dead, as a second Bleeder ripped her left leg clean off. A third Bleeder then attacked the second Bleeder, and a fight ensued between the hairless rats.

The room was soaked in blood, with dismembered bodies scattered into pieces all over the floor.

I shook my head and slammed the door shut. Bleeders were necessary but a complete nuisance.

The further I walked, the darker the castle got, until I had to rely completely on my vampiric ability to see in the dark in order to avoid tripping over the bodies on the ground.

A Bleeder stepped out of a room as I walked by. Upon seeing me, it bowed and covered its bald head as if I was going to hit it. It cowered back into the room.

I continued down the hall of death, the stench of blood causing my fangs to ache.

I entered the elevator and was happy to be leaving the lower castle. Not many humans and supernaturals could handle the transition to vampirism well. They often became mindless, bloodthirsty creatures that disgusted even Skins like me.

The elevator dinged and the strong smell of blood from four stories below disappeared. I stepped out of the elevator and into the red-lit room. Sensual music was playing from hidden speakers while naked Skins mingled among themselves on the floor. Sheer material hung from the ceiling, something I'd always hated. Our queen chose the décor, and she was quite proud of it.

A human woman appeared before me, a thick collar around her neck. She placed her hand on my cheek, her eyes hazy with lust. My gaze followed the chain attached to her collar to the Skin holding it, a woman with pale blonde hair.

I sighed.

The blonde got up and yanked on the chain, causing the human to fall to the ground. "Don't you know never to touch a General?" She hissed at the human.

The woman curled herself around the vampire's leg.

She kicked the human away. The human only returned to latch onto her leg once more, and the vampire smiled.

I walked away.

The blonde placed her hand on my chest. "Are you going to see the queen?"

I turned to her.

She leaned her head back as she stared up at me. "Tell her we miss her. She hasn't joined us in weeks."

A few other vampires nearby mumbled in agreement.

Without warning, I grabbed her hand swiftly and broke it. Her hiss and scream silenced those around us. I turned away without saying a word. The only thing I hate more than Bleeders were these worthless horny Skins.

I finally made it to my destination.

One of the guards standing by the door opened it to give me entrance.

Once inside with the door closed, all sounds from outside vanished. As a vampire with heightened hearing, not being bombarded with the smallest noise was a blessing.

The room was the same as it had always been except for the male and female humans lounging together to the corner.

A young human woman smiled at me, fresh fang marks on her neck.

"General," a soft voice met my ears.

I lowered my eyes to the floor as my queen stepped out from within her closet. "Do you come with good news, my child?"

"She was located by a scouting team but vanished before she could be captured."

She said nothing in response.

Even as I gave no outward sign of my fear… on the inside, I was panicked. This fear only worsened as she walked over to me.

"How?"

I swallowed hard. "Magic—she was with two wolves and a warlock."

She hissed loudly, and the humans began to whimper fearfully.

"But," I added quickly. "Her scent has gotten stronger. She's being tracked as we speak."

She reached a hand out to me and held my face, her long nails scraping my skin.

Despite being 6'3 in height, I had to lean my head back to look up at her.

My vision filled with red as she fixed me in a dead stare. It wasn't just her irises that were crimson. The color engulfed her entire eyeball—pupil, sclera, and iris alike. "That girl holds power that should no longer exist," she said softly. "I shouldn't have to tell you how important it is that she be found before she learns what she is." She leaned closer, her black hair that hung down to her thighs moving forward. "Before she learns to control her power and undo all the hard work we've done to reclaim this earth. Do you understand?"

"Yes, my Queen," I replied and flinched as she released my face but not before one of her nails sliced the skin under my left eye.

I stared at her back as she walked away and swallowed hard as I watched her skin move with her stride. She began removing her silky white dress one thin strap at a time, her skin almost as white as the dress.

The humans started to cry softly, terror in their eyes as her left shoulder suddenly dislocated, and she hunched forward. "Leave me, and don't return without that girl."

I turned and opened the door, as the sound of breaking bones, ripping flesh, and the human's piercing shrieks flooded my senses before the door closed behind me.

Ruby

I was burning up. I wasn't sure why, but I felt like I had been placed inside a furnace as someone was turning up the heat. I slowly opened my eyes, reluctant to be pulled from my slumber. I relaxed again when I understood the reason why I felt so hot.

Xavier's massive leg was draped over my lower body while Axel's arm was over my stomach. Both of them were breathing heavily and emitting more heat than an electric blanket.

Maybe sleeping with both of them had been a bad idea... and yes, we only slept. Still, it was the best sleep I'd had in a very long time. I drifted off to sleep knowing no one on this planet was more protected.

Despite the current state of the world, I was a lucky woman to have these two strong men by my side. Although maybe not so much right now, because if I laid here any longer between them, I might burn to death.

Before getting up, I took a moment to admire them both. On my right laid Axel, my dark knight, with his fire and attitude. Strands of his long hair were covering the side of his face, and I smiled as I remembered our first kiss. Where Xavier and I always shared soft, sweet, slow kisses, kissing Axel had been the complete opposite. Our kiss was deep, passionate, and raw, yet it held the same love I felt with Xavier.

I studied Xavier on my left and sighed. All of this began

because he tried to protect me, and I was happy I had met him. We'd started out disliking each other a little, and then our relationship had grown into something I didn't know was possible. I didn't think a man like him would ever be...my man.

I'd never had someone in my life who always had my back, and I knew I would have that forever in Xavier.

Okay, enough of this, I'm starting to melt.

I untangled myself, which took a lot of effort and patience in order to avoid waking them both.

Eventually, I was on my way downstairs in search of the kitchen.

Once I made it to the first floor, I walked by the spacious living room. When I looked inside, I saw Malcolm's cobra—his shadow demon—pressed against the glass of his cage.

The cobra/shadow demon stopped moving as it caught sight of me and started to turn to smoke.

My eyes widened nervously. "No, fuck no." I started speed walking away from the living room as fast as I could. After a few minutes, I finally made it to the kitchen.

I quickly discovered I had escaped from one demon only to run right into another.

Malcolm sat at the kitchen island with a cup in hand, steam slowly rising from it. "Good morning," he said in a husky morning voice. With the bags under his eyes, it was obvious he hadn't gotten much sleep.

"Good morning," I mumbled under my breath as I walked to the fridge and removed a bottle of water.

"If you wish, I can make you some coffee or tea," Malcolm offered.

I opened my bottled water. "No, thanks. This will do for now."

He nodded and went back to staring into his cup.

I had hoped I'd be alone for a while before I'd have to deal with Malcolm and his ritual. He had said at dawn, and clearly he had meant it.

"How did you sleep?" he asked.

I squinted my eyes at him. "Good. You didn't, I'm guessing?"

He peered up at me before looking back down at his cup. "I want to say I'm sorry about last night. I was insensitive and blind to your pain. You had just watched your mother die and yourself as well," he murmured.

I sucked in a breath, caught off-guard by his apology.

He pushed his cup away, but instead of looking at me, he stared straight ahead. "What I have done—tying myself to that demon, using black magic—has had its negative effects on me. I feel fewer human emotions, and it's only gotten worse over the years."

I closed my water bottle as I listened intently.

He went on, "That's the true price I had to pay. Every day, that shadow demon feeds on my grief from losing Lovette as well as the sadness of losing my only daughter." He looked up at me as he said this.

I gritted my teeth. I wasn't about to say I forgave him. Everything still felt a little too fresh, so I said nothing.

He continued to speak, "It's a price I thought I was willing to pay. The anguish I felt every day at having lost you both threatened to overwhelm me. I was barely hanging on. Having my suffering taken away seemed like a gift at the time, but now, I feel nothing in moments when I should."

"Okay," I said as I pressed a finger against the crease in my forehead. "What was she like?"

Malcolm inhaled and exhaled deeply through his mouth. "Level-headed. Sometimes, annoyingly so." He smiled. "For a woman who possessed her own kind of magic, she was very logical in her thinking and was a lover of science. I guess for her, science and magic were like fraternal twin brothers—similar but not identical. That was the way she looked at it, at least." He gazed at me and his smile grew wider.

I had no idea how to react. Suddenly, Malcolm was this warm, authentic man. Not the one I'd been growing to dislike.

"You have her eyes, gorgeous emerald eyes," he said tenderly.

"And I got your hair," I added.

He chuckled as he ruffled his own hair. "Yeah…" He pulled his cup back to him and looked upward. "We made a beautiful kid, Lovette."

I frowned because I felt sure he'd just said that as if he was speaking to Lovette.

"Sometimes I pretend she's here with me, watching me, hearing me." He took a sip of the contents in his cup. "It helps." He placed the cup back down and sighed. "Loving someone with everything you have can sometimes break you. Do you love them?"

I looked away with a blush. "Um, why?"

"Because they love you, both of them. They feel the mate bond more than you do, I'm guessing."

I nodded. "They do, and I-I do too. Love them, I mean."

He nodded and reached into his pocket.

My heart stopped for a second as he handed me a photo

of Lovette. It was a picture of her at the beach with her dark hair blowing in the wind as she held her beach hat down on her head, her smile wide and radiating joy. I recognized hints of my own smile in hers. My chin began to quiver. It seemed like she'd been an amazing woman, loved by so many. Right now, I could count the people who actually liked me on one hand, and the rest were pursuing me from every direction. How would I ever live up to being her daughter?

"You can keep that. The image from the picture is burned into my brain," he said to me.

I whispered, "Thank you," as I held it to my chest. "I'm ready," I announced.

He frowned.

"I'm ready to continue with the ritual. I want to know everything."

"Okay. This time, whenever you're ready to leave, just say so and I'll end it."

I nodded.

We made our way to the living room, encountering Xavier and Axel on the way.

They stepped back to allow us to proceed.

Now standing inside this circle again, knowing I might see something horrible, my hands shook with fear. "Will you have to cut me again?" I asked.

Malcolm shook his head. "No, that won't be necessary. Just give me your hand."

I looked over at Axel and Xavier just to see their faces before inhaling and giving my hands to Malcolm.

His eyes turned black instantly, and the candles around the circle lit just like before.

The world around us faded away to be replaced by a small bathroom.

My eyes widened as I observed myself at fifteen years old, lying in a bathtub with my wrist slit open. I glanced over at Malcolm.

He looked at me before turning to stare at the pale Ruby of the past, submerged in water up to her chin.

I touched the scar on my wrist. This wasn't how I remembered ever getting it. I thought I had gone through a depressed stage in high school and had cut myself then. This version of events felt foreign.

The past Ruby's eyes were half-open and dazed as she bled out.

Malcolm and I watched as a small floating ball of light appeared in the room.

It drifted to the bathtub and landed on her arm. Ruby gasped and sat up as if she'd been jolted.

All three of us watched as the soft light began to grow until it morphed into Lovette.

The past Ruby began to cry. "It's you, isn't it?"

"Yes, my beautiful girl," Lovette replied, her voice soft but sounding like an echo. "Why did you hurt yourself?"

"I-I did something terrible. I—a girl was bullying me, and I reacted. I-I didn't mean to hurt her, but I reacted and—and…" Ruby looked down at her open wrist and started to cry harder.

I sucked in a breath as I stared at this memory. "This is…"

"…trippy?" Malcolm asked as he finished my sentence.

I nodded. I was looking at my younger self and my dead mother. This was more than trippy.

"I burned her. She just started to burn!" Past Ruby sobbed.

Lovette kneeled beside the tub.

Past Ruby went on as she wept, "I met him. I met my dad right before I saw the girl. He said he was my father, and—I-I was so angry. He left me, all alone, all these years. You left me!"

I was surprised as much as Malcolm when Lovette reached out and was able to touch my past self's cheek.

Lovette took past Ruby's hand and healed the wound on her wrist. "I didn't leave you, sweet girl. I'm always here, always watching, but I can't always appear to you like this. I can't interfere with your life." Lovette tilted her head to the side as she gazed at the past me.

A thought occurred to me as I stared at my mother in this memory. If what she had just said were true, what would it take for me to see her now, in the present?

Lovette spoke to past Ruby, "You're a special girl, Ruby, more than you'll ever know. It's not time for you to die. There is too much left to be done, and you haven't even gotten started."

The past Ruby frowned as she looked from Lovette to her healed wrist and back. "I don't understand?"

Lovette sighed and stood up as she turned to face Malcolm and me. She seemed to be staring right at me.

I made a face and glanced at Malcolm as he peered back at me.

"I'll take your memories of this day. Never spill your blood again, my child, not yet, for your blood is that of the goddess."

"Mom?" I said tentatively as I stepped forward.

Lovette smiled at me—she smiled at *me*—and reached out her hand.

Her image then started to fall away.

Abruptly, Malcolm and I returned to the real world.

"No! No! Send me back!" I screamed.

Xavier and Axel approached me.

I stepped back. *Lovette was speaking to me. She was there!*

Malcolm staggered out of the circle, his eyes wide as he stared at me as if I had just grown a second head.

"Send me back, Malcolm! She was there!" I pleaded.

"How?" he whispered to himself, "How is it even possible?"

I frowned at him. "What is wrong with you? Who cares how? She was right there, *really* there! Let's go back!" I shouted as I stepped closer to him.

He stepped back.

I froze then looked over at Xavier and Axel, who were now watching him with concern as well.

"What's wrong, Malcolm?" Axel asked.

Malcolm stared at him, his eyes still wide with shock. "It —it can't be possible," he stammered.

I stepped back as the cobra appeared out of a cloud of smoke to wrap around Malcolm's neck.

"Malcolm, what the hell is going on?" Xavier asked as he stepped forward to stand protectively in front of me.

The cobra sank its fangs into Malcolm's neck as he went pale, his eyes still black pits. "I think—I think she was saved, b-but how?" Malcolm stated in a weak voice as he pointed at me. "She was saved by the goddess, *your* goddess. She gave Ruby divinity."

THE LUNA RISING UNIVERSE
CONTINUES...

LUNA CHOSEN

Luna Chosen (Book 5)

https://ssbks.com/LR5

Nineteen years ago...

...a mother and her baby died during childbirth.

But two minutes later, that baby *CAME BACK TO LIFE.*

A *miracle,* according to everyone involved...

However, that child grew up to hate her life because it's been nothing but a trip through hell.

Yes, you guessed it. *I'm that child,* Ruby Saunders.

The truth is, at birth my fate was sealed. I was saved by a God, chosen to be a vessel used to save a dying world.

I didn't ask for any of this.

Now after meeting my father the truth about my birth and my power is finally revealed.

I was saved by a *GOD* at birth…given divinity to spare my life.

But…why?

Still the end of the world is upon us as the vampire threat grows stronger…

…and I fear it won't be a pleasant end.

I'm living on borrowed time and…

I fear the life that was spared so many years ago will have to be **REPAID.**
https://ssbks.com/LR5

THE BLOODMOON WARS (A PARANORMAL SHIFTER SERIES PREQUEL TO LUNA RISING)

The Awakening (Book 1)

https://ssbks.com/BW1

The Enlightenment (Book 2)

https://ssbks.com/BW2

The Revolution(Book 3)

https://ssbks.com/BW3

The Renaissance (Book 4)

https://ssbks.com/BW4

The Dawn (Book 5)

https://ssbks.com/BW5

THE VENANDI UNIVERSE

THE VENANDI CHRONICLES

Demon Marked (Book 1)

https://ssbks.com/VC1

Demon Kiss (Book 2)

https://ssbks.com/VC2

Demon Huntress (Book 3)

https://ssbks.com/VC3

Demon Desire (Book 4)

https://ssbks.com/VC4

Demon Eternal (Book 5)

https://ssbks.com/VC5

THE DESTINE UNIVERSE

DESTINE ACADEMY SERIES (A MAGICAL ACADEMY SERIES)

Destine Academy Books 1-10 Boxed Set

https://ssbks.com/DA1-10

HAVE YOU READ THE LUNA RISING PREQUEL?

Click below to get your FREE copy of the **Luna Rising Prequel**.

https://ssbks.com/LunaPrequel

Axel

I'm next in line to be **ALPHA**

...and I'm ready for the challenge.

Focused and determined to make my father proud, I won't let *anything* get in my way.

Until the day I met **HER...**

She's a drop-dead <u>gorgeous</u> blonde with eyes like an aquamarine gem...and she's a witch.

But I'm a werewolf.

And some unions are **FORBIDDEN...**

That little witch has turned my world upside down.

All love comes at a cost.

But this love may cost me *everything…*

https://ssbks.com/LunaPrequel

ENJOY THIS BOOK? I WOULD LOVE TO HEAR FROM YOU...

Thank you very much for downloading my eBook. I hope you enjoyed reading it as much as I did writing it!

Reviews of my books are an incredibly valuable tool in my arsenal for getting attention. Unfortunately, as an independent author, I do not have the deep pockets of the Big City publishing firms. This means you will not see my book cover on the subway or in TV ads.

(Maybe one day!)

But I do have something much more powerful and effective than that, and it's something those publishers would kill to get their hands on:

A WONDERFUL bunch of readers who are committed and loyal!

Honest reviews of my books help get the attention of other readers like yourselves.

If you enjoyed this book, could you help me write even better books in the future? I will be eternally grateful if you could spend just two minutes leaving a review (it can be as short as you like):

Please use the link below to leave a quick review:

http://ssbks.com/LR4

I LOVE to hear from my fans, so *THANK YOU* for sharing your feedback with me!

Much Love,

~Sara

ABOUT THE AUTHOR

Sara Snow was born and raised in Texas, then transplanted to Washington, D.C. after high school. She was inspired to write a paranormal shifter series when she got her new puppy, a fierce yet lovable Yorkshire Terrier named Loki. When not eagerly working on her next book, Sara loves to geek out at Marvel movies, play games with her family and friends, and travel around the world. No matter where she is or what she is doing, she can rarely be found without a book in her hand.

Or Facebook:
Click Here
https://ssbks.com/fb
Join Sara's Exclusive Facebook Group:
https://ssbks.com/fbgroup

Printed in Poland
by Amazon Fulfillment
Poland Sp. z o.o., Wrocław

76793102R00094